THE WICCAN'S ALPHA

THE WICCAN SAGA
BOOK 1

AYLA VOLK

PREFACE

The Wiccan's Alpha is the first book of The Wiccan Saga, a paranormal shifter romance series. For the best reading experience, it is recommended to read this series sequentially. Recommended reading age is 18+.

Content Warning: This novel contains material that might prove to be violent, sexually explicit, or religiously controversial to certain readers.

PROLOGUE

T he beautiful young woman strolled through the bar and sat on the rough leather stool with its fair share of black grunge left on it. She let her thick red curls flow down her exposed back before pulling it to the side and draping it over her lithe shoulder, letting all the gawking men get a glimpse of what was underneath her sleek forest green halter top.

"What will you be having?" The bartender asked as he set a coaster down in front of her.

"Gin and Tonic," she replied in a flirtatious tone.

He was not the one she was after, but she wanted to appear available for when the one she was waiting for showed up. The bartender looked her over and licked his lips before pulling out the bottle of gin from beneath the counter and pouring it into a glass with ice. He topped it off with tonic water and added a lime to the rim, slowly sliding it over to her.

"Thanks," she said, flirtatiously smiling up at him.

"Can I get you anything else?" He was implying something more, such as himself served up in the back room.

"I'm fine," she said with a wink before turning around to face the room.

The bartender waited a moment before moving on to another customer. She scoped out the collection of people inside. A handful of fishermen and a few other day laborers were in for a drink after a hard day's work. One or two were attractive, but most of the others were older than she was looking for.

She had come to Bellingham almost two weeks ago and started her search, scouring several bars and event halls looking for the right target. She was looking for a robust and attractive man with some book smarts. A week ago, she found the perfect mark. A tall man named Jeff who worked as a city planner. His short-cut chocolate brown hair and deep green eyes instantly attracted the woman. After spotting him at the bar, she returned each night to learn his habits. He was a regular there, coming in every evening after work to have a few beers before heading home for the night. After being sure that he was the one she wanted, she dressed herself up and came to the bar ready to lure him to her hotel room.

She waited, eager but nervous. She had only done this once before, four years ago. It was exhilarating and a fun break from her everyday life. For a few days, she could pretend that she was someone else. She thrived on the thrill.

Out of her peripheral vision, she noticed she had caught the eye of another man. He was older. She put him around fifty or so with his greying hair and growing wrinkles. His eyes roamed over her body as if it were a dessert that needed to be consumed. A shiver ran up her spine, and she turned away from him, not wanting to lead him on. She sipped her drink and looked at the clock. The man should be getting off of work about now. He would be there soon, and it would be time for her to work her charms on him.

She polished off her drink before walking to the restroom to freshen up her makeup. She looked in the dirty mirror and applied her brick-red lipstick as she heard the door open. She glanced over and saw the creepy man from the far side of the bar. Her body froze.

"This is the ladies' room," she said sternly, wanting to steer him back the way he came.

"It is?" he replied as if dumbfounded, an obvious rouse.

She turned to look him in the eye, wanting to project as much confidence as she could muster.

"It is, and it's best that you head back out the way you came."

"I will," he said with a cocky smile. "I just happened to see you out there, and what my luck to have stumbled upon you here."

"You mean, after you followed me in?" she stared at him hard.

"Oh, nothing like that. I just got mixed up...but while I'm here, perhaps a lady like yourself is looking for a good time? One I would be happy to help you with."

"No, sorry. I'm not interested. Now leave," she said more forcefully.

"Okay, okay. I get the hint," he raised his hands defensively, yet his voice still unsettled her.

He turned back to the door. The woman's body began to relax with the threat seemingly leaving. That was until she heard the click of a lock. Her eyes widened, and she watched him turn back to face her. There was no more playfulness in his eyes, just a lustful evil that raked down her body.

"Last chance before I scream," she hissed at him.

"The band is starting up. It might be hard for them to hear you, sweetheart. We both know what you came here for. Why don't you just accept that it will be with me, and we can both leave here happy."

He took a step towards her. She dropped her lipstick, throwing her hand up at him. The man who had been standing a good ten feet away from her flew into the door, knocking the air out of his lungs, but he stayed on his feet. He looked at her stunned before turning angry. He stormed at her again; this time, when she threw her hand at him, he jumped to the side, and only his shoulder was struck. He pulled a metal pipe out of his waistband and brandished it against the fearful woman.

She screamed, but as he noted, the band had begun playing. A steady, loud beat reverberated off the walls, muting her sounds outside of the restroom. He neared her, and she tossed her hand once more. The man flew into the sink and fell to the ground.

"You bitch. I was going to make it good for you, but now I will have to make you pay for this."

He pulled himself back up as she ran for the door, continuing to scream out for help. She unlocked the door and began to pull it open when she felt a hard crack in her skull. She fell hard to the ground, squinting her eyes in pain, finding everything a blur. She took in a few deep breaths, trying to gain some composure. Grabbing ahold of the handle to the door, she began pulling herself up, only to be hit again and again.

Her body was riddled with pain, and her mind spun when she felt her pants being undone and yanked down her legs. She tried with everything she had to push her assailant off of her, but with one final hit to the face, her world turned dark, and she felt her life slipping through her fingers. The last thought she had was of her three-year-old daughter, Juniper. With her last living breath, she mustered one last chant to the world.

Le m' anail mu dheireadh, bidh mi a' cur thugad mo phàiste, mo chumhachd agus mo neart gu lèir. Great Selene, ar màthair agus ar dìonadair, cùm sùil air an Juniper agam.

As her prayers to the great Selene to protect her daughter were cast into the universe, she felt the last flicker of her light dwindle and leave her body.

1

Juniper
Nineteen Years Later

I walked through the meadow full of vibrant wildflowers. A mix of floral scents filled my nostrils and brought me a sense of calm and peace. I held my hand out, gliding it across the tops of the plants around me. I glanced to my right and found what I was looking for. I leaned down to inspect the small, beautiful magenta flowers before me. I picked a few stalks of the catchfly flower and added them to the handkerchief inside the satchel that hung around my waist. They had a sticky sap I did not want to clean out of the leather pouch later if it could be prevented. With the increased number of children as of late, we had used our supply and needed to replenish. It worked wonders in promoting a good milk supply. I was happy to volunteer to travel out to the meadow in search of the flowers. After taking my time, I collected a good allotment we would dry upon my return and store until needed.

I strolled back through the thick, lush forest, following the thin trail back to the settlement, stopping once or twice to observe the birds nesting in the nearby trees. I whistled back their tune as if I could speak to them, though they only returned the gestures in my imagination. While I was out, I decided to check the creek beds for algae. Aunt Iris had a fantastic spell she concocted using the slimy green substance that kept your skin as smooth as a baby's. I scraped up a few handfuls worth and slid it into a jar before continuing on my way once more.

"Juniper, where have you been?"

I had just broken off of the trail, coming into the main part of our village, when I heard my best friend Meadow call out to me from across the lush green grass that filled the center of the settlement, a collection of houses and buildings that belonged to the Whisper Creek Coven, my home.

"Hey, Meadow," I replied, smiling at her and picking up my pace so I would not need to shout at her. "I went out to the north meadow to collect some catchfly."

"You should have let me know! I would have gone with you."

"I peeked in your house, but your ma had you busy scrubbing the pots again."

"Ugh, every day! I spend more time cleaning her pots than any other chore."

"So I take it business is good?"

"Yeah, the online sales have been going crazy! And the demand in town has picked up, too," she said.

I laughed at her unamused expression as I started to lead us further into the settlement.

"We all pitch in. She has a great thing going," I tried to encourage her.

"But why do I have to be the dishwasher?" she moaned.

I laughed at her again and let her complain to me as we walked past the cottages that composed our village. I always felt like our little community looked straight out of a fairy tale in one of my childhood books. A simple little village built entirely out of stone and dark timber. Each structure was nestled into the tall trees that made up the surrounding forest. Every house had its own garden out front that was fenced in and accessible through a small wooden gate. The center of our settlement was covered with a sea of deep green grass with little purple flowers scattered throughout. A large fire pit we used for celebrations and gatherings sat centrally, flanked only by a few log benches and picnic-style tables. A small stream flowed over colorful, rounded pebbles to the east of the fire pit, bringing a harmonic, peaceful sound to the area. A little wooden bridge was built over it, connecting the two shores.

Our people were strongly connected to the earth, as we were elemental witches. Here, we could connect to each element and harness its energy. Six families comprised our coven. After fleeing the old country, our great-great-grandmothers all flocked to the northern wildernesses of Washington. They had been chased out by religious groups in the area, having been accused of devil magic, something I didn't even think existed. They knew as soon as they found this land that this was where we were meant to be. They used everything they had to buy the surrounding twelve thousand acres over a century ago, building their first homes by hand, little by little. Each generation added to those original homes, updating and maintaining them along the way. Those buildings still stood and have become home to the family matriarchs, as well as a gathering place for each family and their collection of trinkets and heirlooms. Over time, with our population growing, additional houses were built. Families would build smaller cottages close to their ancestral homes.

Today, there are just over ninety of us, all women, as witches are only born female. Due to this, the women of my coven must take a journey into the human world when they wish to become with child. They cast fertility spells upon themselves and searched for a strong man to impregnate them, disappearing before any attachments could be made or anything beyond a one-night stand could happen. It was not hard to find willing men. Sex seemed to be the only thing on their mind. There were strict rules never to bring one of them back here. This was our safe haven from the outside world, and the elders did not want to bring any bad energy into our space.

We walked up to our family home on the far side of the compound and went inside. The warm air circulating through the room and the strong smell of herbs were like a comforting embrace, welcoming us home. I lived in the main house of our family with my Gran, along with some of my mother's cousins and my Great Aunt Violet. She was the eldest matriarch in the coven and leader of the elders. Most of my cousins lived in separate homes with their mothers or had little cottages where they lived with their children. Had my mother not been murdered when I was only three, I would still be living in our tiny home that sat tucked back into the forest. I have often considered moving there to have some independence, but it would not be approved by the rest of the coven. No one lived alone.

"Ah, Juniper, I'm glad you're back. Were you able to find some catchfly?" my grandmother asked me.

"I did, and I also got some algae while I was out," I said as I set my satchel on the wooden counter in the center of the kitchen and pulled out its contents.

"That's my girl," she said softly, comfortingly.

Meadow and I sat at two stools on the far side of the counter and watched my grandmother walk over and inspect the ingredients I had foraged before preparing them to dry. She bunched the catchfly into small bundles and tied them together with some twine before disappearing into the pantry, where we hung herbs to dry. She returned, added the algae to a jar of liquid, and tucked it into a cabinet. Once everything was stored away, she resumed her original task, kneading dough for bread she was preparing for dinner. I looked over the herbs she had out, noting thyme and rosemary.

"I have some big news!" Meadow nearly shouted.

Both my grandma and I looked over at her excited expression. She seemed as if she would burst if she did not spill the beans soon.

"What is it?" I asked her with a grin.

It was hard not to smile when Meadow was around. Her excited personality filled any room with light and happiness.

"Wren is asking the elders if she can travel!"

My grandmother stopped kneading the dough and asked her, "Does she want a child?"

"Yes! It would be my first niece!"

"That's wonderful news," my Gran smiled, the fine lines of her wrinkles creasing her eyes.

"What about Willow?" I asked about her eldest sister.

She was twenty-eight, two years older than Wren.

"She doesn't care. I don't think she will ever want children."

"Each of us gets to make that choice, Juniper," my Gran added.

I rolled my eyes at the added lesson my Gran felt I needed. I had always wanted a child, but it was encouraged to wait until you were older, at least twenty-five, though a few had their children younger. They wanted us to be fully versed in our skills before venturing outside the settlement. The elders had wards in place to protect us and to keep our gifts hidden from the rest of the world. They feared that we would be driven off our land once again. We were still allowed to go to town every so often, but it usually had to be under the supervision of one of the older generations. I enjoyed going with Heather, Meadow's mother, when she dropped off her shipments. She would allow us to go shopping and even catch a movie from time to time.

Most of the coven shied away from technology, but it was slowly becoming more tolerated. Heather was one of the leading advocates for it, showing the elders how we can use it to profit from their tinctures. She had set up an online company and had a bustling business that most of the coven helped out with now. I liked to think my mother would have been similar to her if she were still alive. My Gran told me stories from when she was young. She was known for constantly pushing the boundaries.

"When is she asking them?" I directed back to Meadow.

"Tomorrow night."

"That's so exciting for her. Does she know where she wants to go?"

"She was thinking Bellingham."

"Not that city," My Gran said as she quickly turned away.

Even though she tried to hide it, I still caught her concern. Ever since my mother's death, she has been wary of larger towns and cities, none more so than Bellingham.

"Magnolia, Bellingham is a safe city," Meadow said, already knowing where her fear stemmed from.

Everyone knew of my mother's demise. She was raped and killed in the bathroom of some dive bar. She had gone to find another suitor. My Gran told me how excited she was to give me a sister with whom I could share my life.

After her death, most were scared to leave our protected lands for a long time. There was even a gap in births. As time went on, though, the urge to have children became too strong, and the women of our coven began going in pairs. After a decade, things finally started to return to normal, and the women who wished to find a suitor would take the journey on their own. They all realized that the process itself was a journey only the individual could pursue. When you traveled in pairs, the other often had too much input or thoughts that interfered, taking away from the experience.

"You may say so, but it will always be the place my daughter was murdered. I will take it up with the elders," she said determinedly as she returned to her kneading.

Her fists pushed the gooey dough roughly. I had never seen her so outwardly angry.

2

Juniper

I walked to the main hall with my long black cloak trailing behind me. The building itself was one of the largest and was located near the center of the settlement. It had a stone base and dark wooden planks for walls, traveling twenty feet up. Large circular windows on either side let the moonlight pour in from the clear night sky. We used the building for gatherings of the whole coven. One of which was the weekly meeting where we came together to discuss updates on the businesses we ran, plan for upcoming celebrations, and let anyone bring issues to the elders, our six leaders. They were the eldest women from each family and were led by the eldest of them all, my Great Aunt Violet.

An eclectic array of wooden chairs was spread throughout the room, filled with women dressed in cloaks similar to my own. At the front sat a table with six padded chairs where the elders sat. I was one of the last in, but found Meadow had saved me a seat beside her. I waved to a few other close friends before Violet, standing from her chair, drew my attention to the front.

"Sisters, we welcome you tonight. Selene looks down upon us with open eyes as she sheds her light and power on us. Let us thank her."

We all stood as she turned and raised her arms to the window, where the nearly full moon proudly showed itself.

"*Màthair, tilg do chumhachd nar cuirp. Bidh sinn a' caitheamh ar beatha dhut.*" We all chanted together.

"Be seated, my sisters."

Everyone took their seats once more. Heather walked up to the front, facing the table.

"I am pleased to inform you that we have made growth in our business. Sales are up in both the town and online. I received an email this week from a company that would like to stock our products in their stores. They are offering us forty percent of the revenue, moving to fifty percent after six months if enough product sells."

Elder Hazel of the Heenan family raised her hand, "That seems like a low percentage. Why can we not get the sixty percent?"

"In my research, forty percent looks on par for what is expected. In a year or two, if our product sells well through their avenues, we should be able to renegotiate to sixty percent. I think this would be a good move for us. We will still have the income from both the store and online, but it would open up a larger market."

"Perhaps it is best to stay in our own coven for business. Things can become problematic if we open up our walls to too many outsiders," Elder Rose of the Kelly family added.

"I agree. But inflation is coming. We have all seen it. We need to be able to protect our land not just with our power but financially. Setting the coven up for future generations should be at the forefront of our concerns. I do not want us to lose our land due to a lack of funds."

The elders whispered with each other before Violet looked at the crowd, "What says the coven?"

"I think it's a smart move," Rowan Nary, my second cousin, added. "I would like to know that my daughter will have the same land and protection I have. The world is changing, and we must accommodate it."

"Does anyone else have an opinion on the matter?" Violet asked.

With uniform silence, she put it to a vote. "All in favor?"

"Aye," everyone's voices chorused through the room.

"Do any oppose?"

Only a few hands raised, followed by their pledge of 'Nay.'

"It seems that most agree. Heather, what would the next steps be?"

"I suggest getting an attorney to help settle the matter. We want to be sure that all of our bases are covered."

Violet grumbled, "I do not like bringing in more people, but if you feel like that is the right step, we will trust you."

Heather smiled proudly before stepping back to her seat.

"Next on the agenda, the full moon is in two days' time. We will have our celebration around the fire as usual. Attendance is mandatory. We must stand together as one to celebrate and thank Selene for her gifts. As with the tradition of the rose moon, we will shower her light with rose petals and delight in the berries of summer. We will need a few volunteers to collect the materials."

Several hands raised, mine included.

"Wonderful. Those of you who have volunteered will meet tomorrow morning at nine, here at the main hall." With all in agreement, she continued, "Does anyone wish to approach the elders?"

I saw Wren raise her hand from the corner of my eye.

"Wren, approach."

She walked to the front, facing the elders just as Heather had.

"I wish to have a child," she spoke confidently.

"Hmm, I see," Violet said, looking her over. "And what about your sister? She would be first in line for the privilege."

Willow stood farther back in the room and joined her sister at the front.

"I do not wish to have children at this time. My sister has my blessing to become with child."

The elders whispered to one another before returning their gazes to them.

"Where do you wish to travel to?"

"My heart calls me to Bellingham, Elder Violet."

"Do you wish to bring someone with you?"

"No, I would like to go alone."

"Stop!" Everyone turned to see my Gran standing from her seat. "She cannot go to Bellingham. It is too dangerous."

Violet's eyes filled with sympathy at her sister's outburst. She stood and walked over to her, holding her hands tightly within her own.

"It has been nearly two decades, sister. It is time to stop living in fear of what may happen and focus on the joy a new life would bring," she said softly but still loud enough for me to hear.

"She can go to another town," Gran said sternly.

Violet ran her hand down my Gran's cheek.

"Oh, Magnolia," she said somberly, "what happened to your Daphne will always bring pain to our hearts. She left this world too soon, only when she wished to bring new life in. We have brought her murderer to justice..."

My eyes shot in their direction. I had never heard more than that she was raped and murdered. How had they brought him to justice?

"We have done our part to rid the world of his evil, returning her soul to Selene. Now, we must allow our young to make their choices. If Wren feels the pull to Bellingham, Selene has made her wishes known. We need to respect that."

I could see a tear prick at the corner of Gran's eye, constricting my chest with sorrow. She had never been able to get over my mother's death. It has been the only unnatural death in our coven since we settled here over one hundred years ago.

"We need your blessing as well, Magnolia," Violet said soothingly.

My Gran stared at her for a moment. I could tell she hated the idea and wanted to protest more, but Violet brought reason to her. She nodded her head as she conceded. Violet helped her sit back down and returned to the elder's table.

"Does anyone else oppose?" Viloet's voice projected.

The room was silent, apart from a stray cricket that had found its way to a hidden crevice.

"Then your request to travel to Bellingham on your own to look for a suitor is approved. We shall see you on the day after the full moon. We wish you the best of luck and a fertile womb."

Wren smiled and returned to her seat along with her sister.

"Anyone else?" Violet asked the room. Without a reply, she stood from her chair. "Let us conclude our meeting around the fire."

She motioned for the doors to be opened, revealing the bonfire outside. Everyone stood from their seats and made their way out. I quickly made my way to Gran to check on her. I grabbed her hands tightly.

"Are you alright, Gran?"

She smiled sadly, "I will be, dear. I think I will rest for a while. You enjoy yourself, and I will see you at home."

I watched as she returned to the Nary house, her shoulders drooping in defeat. My heart went out to her. I was only three when I lost my mother. I remembered the sadness and the looks everyone would give me, but I was too young to comprehend the situation. When I turned twelve, Gran sat me down to tell the story in detail. I was wracked with grief for the whole summer, but I slowly came to terms with it, something she had yet to overcome herself.

3

Juniper

I waited in the main hall for the remainder of the volunteers to show up. I chatted with Clover, one of my friends from the Waldrik family. She was two years younger than me and already itching to have a child.

"I am so excited for Wren! We need a newborn around here. New life brings a breath of fresh air," she said cheerily.

"We have plenty of fresh air around here," I joked back at her, "but I am excited for Wren, too."

"Do you think that they would let me go? To find a suitor, I mean? I would love to have a little babe of my own," she said dreamily.

"I doubt they would allow you to go, at least not for a few more years. You're only twenty, Clover. There is plenty of time to become with child. Right now, it is the time for you to hone your power. Learning to embrace it fully," I replied.

She sighed, "I guess you're right. The youngest mother I have heard of was twenty-three."

"Really?" I asked, surprised.

"Yeah, Amber's mom. She was the youngest mother in the coven."

"Daisy has always had a natural talent with her power. I heard that she could cast an evocation spell by sixteen," I whispered.

"Wow! I never want to get on her bad side," Clover's eyes widened.

"Me either," I laughed.

At that moment, Daisy entered the room, and our smiles fell. She approached us with a mischievous look on her brow.

"Did I hear someone talking about me?" She asked in her sing-song voice.

"No!" We both shouted.

"Oh...Okay," she eyed us knowingly before smiling and moving to the group's center. "Everyone, gather over. I need two groups. One to head to the north meadow to find the wild roses and the other to travel down the south river to collect berries."

I quickly raised my hand. "I'm happy to do the roses."

"Berries, it is for you."

My mouth was agape from her opposition to my request. Usually, we get to go to whichever task we volunteer for. I knew instantly that this was a repercussion for talking about her. Witches were tightly bonded to their coven sisters, but they were mischievous and would rectify any wrongdoings without a second thought. I had been caught, so I had to pay the price.

"Yes, Daisy," I said, admitting defeat.

She smiled at me and directed the remaining women to their respective roles. We left together, the two groups heading in opposite directions once outside. I enjoyed picking berries, but not as much as strolling through the rainbow-colored wildflowers in the meadow. We walked for nearly an hour before we found our first strawberry patch. With baskets in hand, we quickly went to work gathering all of the ripened berries. I slipped one in my mouth, savoring the sweet flavor that burst along my tongue.

"Juniper Nary, I know you did not eat a ceremonial berry," Cedar Heenan quipped.

I quickly turned, licking away the evidence on my lips.

"Just testing the product," I smiled back.

We both broke out in a fit of laughter.

"They are quite good," I said as we returned to our duty, "You should test one as well."

She eyed me mischievously before biting into a large, juicy one.

"Yum! These are good. I'm excited to eat the rest tomorrow," she said as she wiped the juice from her chin.

I moaned in excitement, "Me too."

After several more hours, we finally returned home, dropping the berries off at the main hall. Those who had volunteered for the ceremony would wash and prepare them. I said farewell to the others and walked home, enjoying the cool, gentle breeze. When I walked through the door, Heather was sitting cross-legged on the sofa, typing away on her computer. She looked up from the door closing, meeting my eyes.

"Oh, good! Juniper, come here for a minute."

I walked over, picked up a pillow, and plopped on the sofa next to her, holding the pillow to my chest.

"I need to go to town the day after tomorrow to meet with the attorney. I was wondering if you and Meadow would like to go with me?"

"Really?" I asked excitedly.

"Yes. So do you?"

"Of course!" I replied, throwing myself at her and pulling her into a tight hug. "That would be amazing, but why do you want us there?"

She pulled back from our hug and adjusted the computer in her lap, "Well, for one, you know the elders prefer us to travel in pairs, and two, I want to teach you guys the business. Someone will have to take over for me one day."

"I would be honored. Thank you for thinking of me."

"You two are my little adventurers," She bumped my shoulder with hers.

"Have you already told Meadow?"

"Yeah. She's at our house doing the dishes."

I held back another laugh at Meadow's endless chore. She really couldn't get away from it.

"I'll go talk to her," I said, standing quickly.

"Oh, while you're down there, will you two whip up a batch of calming lotion? It's been selling like hotcakes online."

"Sure thing."

"And make sure you wash the pot out when you're done."

I turned and saluted her before I raced back outside. Their home was the closest to the main Nary house, just down a small trail to the west. As I approached, I could hear music blaring from the open window, and Meadow was singing along at the top of her lungs.

I opened the door to their kitchen and shouted over her music, "Meadow! We're going to town!"

She dropped the pot she was washing into the sud-filled sink and started jumping up and down, "I know! How awesome is this?"

We danced around the room, celebrating. It was rare to leave the coven grounds. When we traveled with Heather, we only left once a month, at the most. Some of the others were almost never able to go. I was thrilled that I was one of Heather's go-tos when she went. We started pulling out the ingredients to make the lotion Heather had requested.

"Do you think she will let us catch a movie?" Meadow asked as she strained the herbs out of the mix.

"I hope so. Did you see the new chick flick that's out?"

"Yeah. That looks good. Maybe she will go with us."

We both crossed our fingers, hoping we could explore a little.

4

Juniper

"Juniper, we're leaving," Gran called up the stairs.

"Coming," I called back, throwing my cloak over my shoulders.

I didn't mind the cloak, but we wore it so often, and in the summer, it was hot. I tugged at the hood a few times, encouraging the air to flow in before heading out of my door to join the others. We approached the center of the settlement to find a gorgeously decorated get-up. The girls had strung lights on the posts that circled the raging bonfire. Rose petals covered the ground, matching the roses woven with the lights. A table full of mouth-watering food sat to the side, and other tables had been set up for us to enjoy our feast. I saw Meadow and Cedar on the opposite side of the flames and checked in with Gran before heading over.

"Hey, Ladies. Fancy meeting you here."

"Yes, what on earth are you doing here?" Meadow played back.

"And look, we're even wearing the same thing. What are the chances?"

We all laughed.

"Time to eat," Someone called from the tables.

We walked over and found a place in line, chatting about our trip the following day to town.

"I need to get on Heather's good side so she will take me with her sometime," Cedar complained.

She was always jealous when we got to go into town.

"Sorry, spots are already taken," Meadow teased her.

We picked up our plates and served ourselves food. I took a good helping of strawberry barbecue chicken, a strawberry pasta salad, and, of course, sliced strawberries. There were several other non-strawberry foods, but we indulged when it was the rose moon. We sat together at the table, laughing at each other's jokes, and sipped on the strawberry liquor that Clementine Murphy had made. It was sweet and delectable, and it was easy to go overboard without realizing it.

After a good helping of strawberry desserts, Violet gathered everyone's attention. "It is time."

We all stood and circled the fire.

"*Bidh sinn a 'dòrtadh nan ròsan ort Selene. Tha sinn a' tairgse dhut toradh ar saothair.*"

She chanted before dropping her cloak, revealing her nude body underneath. Though Violet was eighty-six, a healthy supply of youth spells made her look no older than fifty. Stark silver hair and crow's feet could be seen, but she was fit enough to turn some heads. We recited her chant, each dropping our cloaks after her. There we stood, all ninety-one of us in our naked beauty, dancing under the full moon. It is a cliche of witchcraft, but one we embrace.

We soaked up the power that Selene bestowed upon us through the moon. I felt free and strong, as if I could run across the globe. I could feel the power coursing through my blood. The more we danced, the stronger it became. Paired with the strawberry liquor, it was not long before the tricks came out. Someone turned Poppy's hair bright orange. She cursed out those closest to her before reciting her own incantation to turn it back to the auburn it naturally was. A few others had made the roses on the ground take root, growing large thorn shrubs in the middle of our dance floor. I looked at my Gran, who seemed free from her earlier worries. It was as if her youth was brought back to her under the moonlight.

As the night faded and the first pricks of sunlight threatened the sky, everyone dispersed to their homes, ready for a good night, well, morning, of rest.

"Juniper, if you are not down here in five minutes, we are leaving without you!"

I jumped awake, running a hand through my curly red mop of hair. My head ached, and I held it still momentarily before realizing what Heather shouted up the stairs.

"Shit!" I said as I flew out of bed, grabbing the closest pair of jeans and a shirt.

I raced down the steps, finding Heather and Meadow looking me over and stifling their laughter. I squished my nose at them, silently telling them to keep it to themselves as I slipped on my shoes and followed them down the trail. We did not have many uses for cars, but we always had a couple for everyone to use. I sat in the back of the light blue 2010 Nissan Xterra and buckled up.

"Why on earth would you schedule the meeting the morning after the full moon?" I asked Heather.

"It's the first time they had," she shrugged her shoulders.

I ran my fingers through my hair as I tried to unknot the rat's nest that had formed overnight. The bumpy dirt road gave way to smooth pavement as we got onto the country highway, quickly making our way to town. We pulled up in front of an old house with a sign out front that read *George E. Jones, Attorney at Law*. The yard had been converted into a small parking lot, which we pulled into. We walked up the concrete pathway to the front porch that had a bright white wooden railing wrapping around it. There was a doorbell to the side, which Heather pressed. A chime could be heard from inside. A curtain on the bay window to our side pulled back, revealing an older man with a white beard and equally white hair that had been combed back. He waved at us and made his way to the door, letting us in.

"Hello, you must be from Boutique of Botanicals."

"Yes, I'm Heather. We spoke on the phone the other day," she said, extending her hand to shake his.

"Yes. Welcome."

"And this is my daughter, Meadow, and my niece, Juniper."

It was not uncommon for us to tighten the blood relationship when speaking to others. It was complicated to explain that I was, in fact, her first cousin, once removed. Besides, most of us, or at least those in the same generation, referred to each other as cousins, no matter the distance.

"It's a pleasure to meet you, " he replied. "Why don't we take a seat in my office?"

He gestured to the room to the right of the door. I assumed it used to be either a sitting room or a dining room when the building still served as a residence. At the center was an elaborate wooden desk with two chairs facing it. In the corner was another chair that had been pushed to the side. Behind his desk and flanking the window were large built-in bookshelves full of law books.

"Let me get this for you, Juniper," he said as he pulled the spare chair up to the desk.

We watched as he walked around the desk, taking his seat in his tall leather executive chair, which leaned back from his weight. He straightened the papers scattered in front of him and placed them in a folder, closing it and sliding it to the side.

"Let's see here," he said as he grabbed another file from under the stack on the corner.

He opened it, flipping through a few pages before setting it back down, and began, "I contacted World Mart and had them fax over their proposal. I've looked it over, and it looks good. Do you already know the revenue distribution?"

"Yes. If the sales are good, I was wondering if we could add something about us getting sixty percent after eighteen months."

"We can add that and see if they accept it. I think it is a good amendment to add in."

"When I talked to them on the phone, they asked to have a final meeting in person at their headquarters in Vancouver. It's not too far from here. I would be happy to join you, but I would need to charge for travel expenses."

"I think we can handle that. I would rather you be there to talk to them in person."

"Alright, then. Let's walk through a few logistics with the contract, and then I will call them after I correct the revisions."

Mr. Jones blurted off a bunch of legal mumbo jumbo that I struggled to understand, but I still tried to pay attention. Currently, we are set to have a two-year contract with them. They wanted us to be exclusive, but Heather told him that we still wanted to be allowed to sell on our own website and in town at the local vendors that we use. She didn't want to burn any bridges with our current relationships, and we made good money directly from our website. By the end of the meeting, my head was swimming with the numbers and legalities associated with the contract. Now I understand why Violet was hesitant to partner with outside companies. It became complicated.

We walked back out to the car, standing outside it and stretching our legs before getting in.

"Hey, mom," Meadow said, "how about we give these old noggins a break from whatever that was and go check out the newest rom-com?"

Meadow raised her eyebrows a few times, trying to entice her.

Heather laughed, "That was a lot, wasn't it? I guess we could use a break after that. I could check in on the store while I'm in town and see if they need any resupply. I'll give you girls some money while I run around. I'll meet you at the diner after."

Meadow hugged her and pulled the money out of her hand just as Heather pulled it from her purse.

"Thanks, Mom!" She shouted, grabbing my hand and running towards Main Street.

5

Juniper

S ince the full moon had passed and we were still waiting to hear back from Mr. Jones, life had returned to normal. Meadow and I were collecting the herbs needed to make Heather's next product, some love lotion. While her concoctions were mostly herbs and tinctures, she liked to add a light spell into them here or there. She had told us that the love lotion would have an attractant spell where the wearer's interests would respond if they matched and were not already spoken for. She said it was a bit complicated since she didn't want to mess with some-one's life, but she also wanted to help pull hearts together. Both Meadow and I eyed her suspiciously.

"At least tell us that you will trial-run it before spreading it to the mass market?" I egged her.

"Of course. I have a few people in town that I would like to see what happens."

"No wonder everyone eats these up, Mom. You're putting love spells on them."

"No. Not love spells, attractant spells. Think of it as a boost of confidence. They have to like each other already for it to work."

"Sure," We both said, rolling our eyes and smiling at her.

We heard her phone ring from the main room. There were only a few phones in the settlement—one at each main house—and Heather had her own since she ran a major business. She walked over and picked it up, speaking quietly. It was hard to hear what she was saying over the running water in the sink. We watched her as she came back in, waiting to see if it was Mr. Jones.

"Well...?" Meadow urged.

"We are meeting them next week in Vancouver."

"We?" I asked.

"All of us, if you two are still interested in coming."

"Yes!" We both screamed, jumping up and down, hugging each other with our soapy hands.

WE LOADED our luggage into the car before turning back to the coven, which had congregated around us to say farewell. My Gran approached me and pulled me into a tight hug. I could tell this was hard for her. If she thought Bellingham was bad, what would she think of me going to one of the largest cities in Canada? I think the only reason she even agreed was that there would be three of us.

"Bye, Gran," I muffled into her shoulder.

"Bye, my sweet child," her comforting voice wrapped around me.

I stepped back and squeezed her hands once more before I looked over my shoulder and saw Heather hugging Wren, who would be leaving at the same time. Rather than the small overnight bag each of us was toting, she had several large suit-cases, enough for the month she was allowed to be gone. We would caravan to Bellingham and get her situated before finishing our trek to Vancouver.

Heather had found us a cabin to stay in north of the city. The elders were too concerned for us to be in the heart of it. It looked idyllic in the images she had shown us. Standard to the Pacific Northwest, it had mossed over grey shingle siding with large logs supporting it on a steep hillside. A thick, lush forest surrounds it. It added an hour to our drive, but having Gran feel more at ease made me happy about it. We will be able to see the city more tomorrow morning when we go to the meeting. We would stay two nights to avoid driving back in the dark. Meadow and I were equally excited about this trip. Neither of us had ventured farther than the nearby town.

Violet hugged Wren and whispered in her ear before stepping back and allowing her to climb into her own car. Heather would ride with her until we arrived in Bellingham, where she would spend time with her daughter before continuing on with us.

"Bye, Mom. Thank you for trusting us with this," Heather told Violet, hugging her as well.

I buckled into the driver's seat and rolled away from the settlement. As we passed the protective wards, we felt a tingle in our skin, letting us know we were officially off of coven land.

"Road trip!" Meadow shouted beside me as she turned the radio on and blared music.

I laughed and joined in, weaving through the narrow dirt road to the highway. The drive was a few hours, but the non-interrupted time chatting and singing with Meadow felt like it flew by. Before we knew it, we had arrived in Bellingham. We gawked at the size of it. Only in movies and magazines had we ever seen a city or a building more than two stories tall, for that matter. Heather had a few minor panic attacks trying to circumvent the traffic, but overall, she did well. It helped that we followed her, and she ensured that we stayed right behind her.

We pulled up in front of a quaint, tiny home on the outskirts of Bellingham. It had an arched roof that overhung the small front porch, held up by a few simple columns. Either side of the door had a small picture window with white drapes hanging inside.

"It's a short-term rental. You can rent them for a few days or a month. Mom set it up so she has the place to herself for the whole month. It's close to the police station, too." She laughed at the last part.

"Got to keep her baby safe, right?" I said, pinching her cheeks together.

She pulled her head back and squished her face together in rebellion of my teasing. We unbuckled and exited the car, meeting Wren and Heather in front of the house. Heather pulled a small piece of paper from her pocket and handed it to Wren.

"It says that there is a...smart lock on the door. Whatever that is."

She walked up and inspected the keypad lock on the entry before glancing back at the paper in Wren's hand. Typing in the numbers, I heard a quiet beep before the light turned green, and I heard a mechanical sound as the lock turned.

"Well, isn't that fancy?" She laughed, opening the door.

Inside, the furniture was modern but simple. To the left, there was a small sitting area with a love seat across from two white lounge chairs. A flat-screen television sat against the wall on a sleek black cabinet. Meadow and I hauled in Wren's luggage and found the bedroom in the back, dropping it off there. When we returned to the main living area, we found Heather going through the kitchen cabinets.

"Let's run to the grocery store real quick. I want to be sure you know where it is and that you get some healthy food," she exaggerated the last part. You girls stay here until we return and do not open the door for anyone. Do you hear me?"

"Yes, yes. Go on," I said, ushering her out the door.

"And pick me up some snacks, please!" Meadow shouted after them.

We both laughed and plopped onto the loveseat in the main room.

"You're going to drive your mom mad on this trip."

"Yeah, but she loves me."

"Of course she does. Doesn't mean she won't hit you on the back side of your head, though."

She faked a scared face before leaning forward and grabbing the remote off the table. We both inspected it. We had some technology at the coven, but television was not among them. She clicked the power button, and we watched the screen come to life. A nature show depicting life in Yellowstone National Park came up. Instantly captivated, we cozied into the comfy loveseat and were mesmerized by the images shared with us.

We watched as a herd of elk nipped away at the ground. The buck lifted its head, sporting a full rack of antlers, as it noticed movement to its side. A massive brown bear made its attack, chasing down its prey.

"Run, little elk!" Meadow shouted from next to me, making me jump.

I grabbed one of the throw pillows and swatted her with it.

"Don't do that!"

"What?" she asked, surprised.

I shook my head at her and tuned back into the show. Just when I thought the bear would take the elk down, a pack of wolves descended, chasing off the bear and claiming the kill as their own. The image of the wolves tearing away at the elk made my stomach churn, yet there was something hypnotizing about them. The way that they worked together to ward off the larger predator. It kind of reminded me of home. As a coven, we were more powerful than any single witch. That is why we created covens—strength in numbers.

I had started to fall asleep against Meadow's shoulder when we heard the lock turning. Both of us shot upright and stared as Heather and Wren returned with several paper bags of groceries. They looked at our faces before shaking their heads and heading to the kitchen to put the food away.

"Alright, honey. If you need anything, just call," Heather said, handing Wren a cell phone.

Another rarity at home. All of our phones were landlines.

"What if you're not near the phone?" she asked worriedly.

"I programmed all of the coven numbers in. Just call until someone picks up."

She hugged and kissed her on the cheek before climbing into the passenger seat of our car. We waved goodbye as we drove down the quiet neighborhood road.

"Are you alright?" Meadow asked her mom from the driver's seat.

We could see the worry on her face.

She gave a weak smile back at her, "Yes. It's just hard to trust the world with your children."

We drove in silence for a while after that. It was a weird concept, leaving her behind. We always stuck together. I had never been alone for more than a few hours in my entire life. I couldn't imagine an entire month on my own.

6

Juniper

"Just up this road," Heather said, pointing to a well-worn dirt road to our right.

We watched as the forest rolled by, not seeing any sign of structures. As we turned a bend in the road, the cabin from the pictures Heather had shown us came out of nowhere. It really was secluded.

We each climbed out of the car and stretched our sore, stiff muscles. I'd concluded that I would rather wash all of Heather's pots for a week than stay cooped up in a car like that again. My body needed to move. We walked inside the cabin and took in the rustic features. Everything was made out of wood, even the walls.

"Guess they went all out on the wood cabin feel," Meadow joked, inspecting a small wooden bowl by the door.

"You can say that again," I replied.

"Okay, there are two bedrooms. You girls can stay in the one with the two twin beds. But you must promise not to keep me awake at night with all your giggling. Otherwise, I will boot one of you down to the couch."

"Yes, ma'am," we said in unison.

Heather sighed at us as she took her bag up the wooden stairs and found her bedroom. Meadow and I looked at each other and held in the laughter that threatened to spill out. We made our way upstairs, finding our room. The walls were decorated with images of wolves, while the table between the beds was a carved log in the shape of a bear holding up the glass pane on top. Even the lamp was a bear hugging a tree stump.

"Do you think there's a television at least?" Meadow asked, looking around the room.

"I didn't see one."

She sighed. "Well, it's good I brought one of my books with me."

She plopped down on the bed, moving the pillows to support her head.

"I'm going to go look around outside. Do you want to come with me?"

"No, thanks. I'm good here."

I didn't know how she could just sit there and read when there was a brand-new place to explore. I walked out to the small hallway and found Heather in her room, digging through her bag.

"Heather, do you want to go for a walk? I need to stretch my legs."

"No, sweetie. I need to review the contract again before the meeting tomorrow morning."

"Okay," I said, shrugging my shoulders. "Looks like I'm on my own."

"Don't go too far. It will be dark soon, and I don't need you getting lost in the woods."

"I won't," I smirked at her overprotective nature.

I grabbed my jacket on the way out and found a small trail

behind the house. The late afternoon sun fought its way down past the mass of branches that towered over me. Ferns and moss clung to the sides of the trail, desperate for their need for sunlight. I ran my hand over the top of a few nearby, savoring the energy they released. I could hear the slight babble of water close by and wandered off the trail to find it.

Just over a small hill, the creek I was searching for showed itself. I walked down and found a large, dark grey rock to sit on nearby. I slipped my shoes off and dipped my toes in the frigid water. Even in June, the water felt like it was one step away from ice, but it was amazing after a day of travel. I leaned back on my arms, enjoying my time in a new place and observing the surrounding area. Besides the slow call of the water, it was surprisingly quiet. No birds or other animals called to their kin.

I decided to dry my feet and continue on the trail for a little longer. As I slipped my foot into my shoe, I heard the crack of a small twig nearby. My eyes darted in the direction from which it came. Thick ferns blocked my view of whatever it was, but something inside me pulled me towards it. I quickly pulled on my other shoe and stood, looking for the easiest way to cross. The creek was not large, but I did not want to have wet shoes for the rest of our trip. There was a log ten feet down water that I walked to, steadying myself as I crossed, my arms out for balance.

I neared the ferns from which the sound had come and gently moved them aside, finding nothing. Perhaps it was a rabbit that ran away when I crossed. I looked around, still feeling a pull. I weighed whether I should continue searching for whatever drew me to it, but remembered Heather's words not to get lost. I pouted my lips in frustration before returning to the log and crossing back over.

I could see night weighing in and decided to head back to the cabin. There was no need to venture into this dense forest in the dark, especially since the trail was not well-marked. I found my way back on the same path I had come in on until the faint lights from the cabin could be seen ahead. I looked back from where I came, still feeling a pull. Whatever it was, I would have to find it tomorrow after the meeting.

I walked inside to a room full of the delicious scents of Heather's cooking. She had made us stop in the city for groceries of our own. I didn't complain because I knew she would cook some good grub for us while we were away.

"Just in time for dinner," Heather chimed as I sat at the table in anticipation. "How was your walk?"

"It was great. It's beautiful around here. Thicker forest than at home."

"No kidding. I couldn't even see the cabin until we were practically inside," Meadow grunted as she piled a good helping of turkey meatballs on her plate.

"I found a nice little creek to dip my toes in."

"Nothing like a little water energy to spruce you up," Heather said enthusiastically between bites.

"It was weird, though. There was something that called to me out there..."

My thoughts wandered back to the pull I had felt. I rubbed my chest at the memory.

"Not another one of your bird friends, was it?" Meadow goaded me.

I pursed my lips and looked back from the window, realizing I had been staring out. I looked at the others and noticed Heather watching me intently. She pursed her lips but said nothing else. I was thankful she didn't want me to explain further. I really didn't know how to describe it.

7

Juniper

I stood exhausted at the door, waiting for Meadow to hurry up and get in the car. We had an hour's drive to the World Mart office. I kept looking at the surrounding forest, willing it to reveal its secrets. I could barely sleep last night due to constant tossing and turning. I had to fight myself not to venture back into the woods to find whatever pulled at me. I realized that it was my soul calling out, a feeling I had tried to tune into over the years. Perhaps this trip would enlighten me further, allowing deeper insight within myself. All I knew for sure was that I would most definitely be going for another walk when we returned.

"About time," I practically shouted at Meadow as she casually strolled down the stairs.

"Don't hate the beauty, Juniper."

I rolled my eyes at her and followed her to the car, where Heather was already buckled into the driver's seat.

"Let's do this, ladies!" she said excitedly.

I was glad to be in the back seat today. Meadow had offered me the front passenger seat, but I was too lost in my thoughts to hold a conversation. The back seat was my sanctuary from Heather's frazzled mind and Meadow's comical onslaught. They were two of the closest people to me after Gran, but sometimes, a girl needed a break to get lost in her own mind.

I watched as the forest gave way to neighborhoods and, eventually, the city. It was so densely packed that I nearly felt like I couldn't breathe. Every part of me wanted to return to the cabin and go for the walk I had promised myself. I clenched my fists, fighting the urge to yell at Heather to turn us around.

We finally pulled up in front of a towering skyscraper. A parking structure was attached to it, which we had been instructed to park in. After several levels of searching, Heather squeezed our car into a tight spot, and I quickly jumped out, desperate to find fresh air. Instead, I was choked by the amount of pollutants. You could taste the exhaust floating all around. Witches were more sensitive to pollutants than other people. I looked over at the others and saw them wrinkle their noses at the same sensation.

We took an elevator in the parking structure down and entered a lobby. It had the highest ceilings I had ever seen, with massive columns supporting them near the windows. One lone potted tree sat in the corner and reached toward the windows with its branches in search of freedom. Mr. Jones stood central in the massive space and called us over.

"I will do most of the talking. If you feel like something needs to be changed or addressed, you can either write it down on my notepad or whisper it in my ear," he briefed us as we talked in the corner of the lobby.

Heather stopped and looked at him.

"I appreciate your tactics, Mr. Jones, but I will speak for myself. You are here to ensure they don't get one over on us."

His charming smile quickly replaced a look of surprise.

"Of course, Ms. Nary," he said through that forced smile.

We rode the elevator up to the thirtieth floor and made our way to the reception desk.

"How may I help you?" A small woman with dyed blonde hair with dark roots asked as we entered the glass doors.

"Uh, yes. We are here for a meeting with Mr. Sharp. We are from Boutique of Botanicals."

She smiled at us and stood. "Let me show you to the conference room. They have had brunch brought in from a fabulous restaurant down the way. May I offer you a beverage while you wait?" she asked, opening another glass door to a room with a large table surrounded by fancy black leather task chairs.

"Water is fine," Heather smiled at her.

"Coffee for me, thanks," Mr. Jones added.

"And how about you two?" She directed at Meadow and myself.

"Water," we both replied, unsure of ourselves.

I was impressed by how well Heather held herself here. It was as if she was made for this sort of thing. I, on the other hand, felt so out of place. Everything here was unnatural and fake. It made me itch. I was always happiest when surrounded by nature, lost in the world around me. We watched the petite woman walk confidently away, returning a short while later with our drinks. She set a bowl of lemon wedges nearby.

"In case you would like lemon with your water," She gestured.

"Thank you," I said, forcing a smile of my own.

My cheeks would be sore by the end of this meeting. I watched several people walk past us, giving us the occasional glance. Each one was dressed in suits and other business attire, while the three of us wore our standard loose skirts and peasant tops. I guess you could say we were a bit hippyish. I had questioned whether to wear my jeans today, but at least the skirt felt slightly more formal. Better than our nakedness, we often paraded around in. The thought of us sitting here in only our bare skin made me grin.

A tall, intimidating man walked in with the same forced smile I had seen with every other person we encountered in the city. Several other people, two men and a woman, followed after him, taking their seats directly across from us.

"Welcome to World Mart headquarters. We are glad that you were able to make the journey."

"Of course," Heather replied without hesitation.

We spent several hours going back and forth over the deal and contract. They had agreed to all of Heather's terms. I could feel her sense of accomplishment rolling off her in waves. I, myself, fought the urge the entire time we were in there to flee the building back to the forest where I could finally breathe, but I held strong, never giving any sign of my struggle. On the other hand, Meadow was a fidgeting mess the whole time. Heather eventually rested her hand on her leg underneath the table and whispered what I can only assume was a calming spell on her.

We exited the elevator and said our goodbyes to Mr. Jones. Even though Heather had done all the negotiating, he seemed pretty pleased with himself. The coven was lucky to have her. Once we were back in the car, returning to the cabin, I took my first real breath since we had left.

"How do you guys think it went?" She asked as she navigated the dirt roads leading back to the cabin.

"Can I just say you are such a badass, Mom!" Meadow praised.

"Thank you, honey. Honestly, I was a bit nervous in there." Her voice gave away her excitement.

"It never showed," I smiled at her, catching her eyes in the review mirror.

As Heather and Meadow walked inside the rustic cabin that was our home for one more night, I turned back to the thick forest, feeling the pull even more potent.

"I think I am going to take another walk," I said quickly.

Heather stopped and peered back at me as if she were trying to analyze me.

"Do you want me to come?" she asked after a moment.

"Do you mind if I go on my own? It was a lot being in the city," I replied quickly.

I wanted to explore, and I knew something awaited me within the trees' depths. It felt personal, and while I enjoyed spending time with Heather, this seemed like something I needed to do on my own.

A soft smile came to her face in understanding. "Of course, dear. Just be back before dark."

"I will," I said, turning back to the enchanting greenery in front of me.

8

Juniper

I walked hastily back down the same trail as the day before. Noticing the small hill to my side and the familiar sound of the creek, I walked over to it, finding the same rock I had sat on. I slipped my shoes off and dipped my toes into the water, feeling a rush of energy pulse through my body.

I sat waiting for the same crack of a twig, but it never came. Deciding that I would walk the trail a little further, I slipped my shoes back on and headed back to the trail. It serpentined through the ever-thickening forest until it opened up to a stunning meadow, lush with wildflowers reminiscent of home. A smile took hold of my face as I wandered off the trail, running my fingers over the top of the tall grasses and flowers. I had neared the other side when I heard rustling behind me. I turned and found a large black wolf staring me down. Though surprised to see the creature, I was not scared. The pulse inside of me that had been tugging at every one of my nerves blasted through me, making me feel like this was where I was meant to be.

I looked into the wolf's dark black eyes, only to get lost in them. I reached my hand out, offering it to smell like one would do with a dog. It cocked its head to the side as if it was surprised by my movements. I took a step forward, only for it to take a step back. We watched each other for what felt like an eternity, but all I wanted to do was rush up, wrap my arms around its thick neck, and nestle into its fur, no matter how much I tried to bring reason into my brain. That this was a dangerous wild animal, and I couldn't. It felt like we were connected somehow. I took another step forward, but it did not retreat this time.

"Come here," I called to it.

It took a step back and dropped its head below the grass. I heard a loud crack as if someone had broken a bone. Worried, I approached quickly, only to be faced with a man only dreams could make up. He stood himself up, revealing his sculpted body and dark eyes. He had thick, short black hair that looked as if he had just woken up. Had he been asleep in the grass this whole time? Where had the wolf gone? None of this made sense.

I stopped and inspected him, realizing that he wore no clothing. My eyes traveled down his washboard abs, stopping on his large appendage, which stood proudly in front of him. Is this what a man looks like? What was I thinking? Of course, it is. Here is one now, standing in front of me. I looked back up at his face, noticing the smirk he sported.

"Like what you see, mate?" His deep voice resonated within me.

I was speechless. I had just been caught gawking at a man's cock. I had heard the stories from my cousins. I knew what it was and what it was used for, but to see one in person was... I shook the thoughts from my mind, reaching his eyes with my own once more. They were entrancing, like a siren's call that pulled me in.

He took a step towards me, sending a shiver up my spine. I still could not speak but watched this Adonis of a man approach me as if I were a sweet he desired. When he was only a breath away, he reached out, taking my hand. Sparks and a tingling sensation coursed through my body, making me feel weak in the knees and melting the world around us away. He wrapped his strong arm around me, steadying me so I did not tumble to the earth.

"What is your name?" he asked, his tone gentle.

Finally pulling myself out of my trance, I replied. "J-Juniper. What is yours?"

"Forest."

One word. That is all it took to feel as if my heart would explode with fulfillment.

"Forest," I repeated as if it were the sweetest word known to man.

It was a word I had spoken thousands of times before, but to say it like this, for his name...there was something so much more to it, as if the word itself had gained a whole new life, a purpose within my soul.

"You do not smell of wolf to me, yet not quite human. What are you?"His inquisitive voice was filled with hesitation.

Taken aback by his questioning, I looked at him, puzzled, "What do you mean?"

His gaze turned serious as if I had insulted him. I took a step back, sobering up from the encounter.

"Are you a human?" his tone was more stern.

Did he know that I was a witch? Would he hunt me down if he knew? I took another step back, freeing myself from his hold. I shifted my feet so I could make a run for it if the situation came.

"What are you?" I asked accusingly, my hand coming to my hip.

"I'm a wolf. You saw me shift, yet you were not afraid," he replied. His voice held a lick of contemplation as he spoke.

"A-A wolf?" I stuttered.

The realization that the man in front of me had transformed

into what he was now from the wolf I had seen earlier took me by surprise. I had seen it with my own eyes. The wolf lowered into the grass, and Forest emerged, but I had been too enchanted by him even to put two and two together. What was I supposed to feel right now? Shock? Fear? I dug down deep within myself to realize that neither was the answer. He was who I was connected to, this man in front of me. I looked him over as if it would reveal all the secrets I was looking for, but none came.

"I am a witch," I answered honestly.

His shoulders tensed from my confession. He was a witch hunter! He would send me to my death in an instant. I looked back towards the forest, seeking its sanctuary. I debated whether I could make the distance before the man, but I knew the wolf would take me, sending me through death to where I had come from. I looked back at him, fear evident on my face. As if reading my mind, he held his hands up non-threateningly.

"Wait," he said softly. "I won't hurt you. I could never hurt you. I was just surprised. I've never met a witch before."

I watched him cautiously in case it was a trap. For how much my brain wanted to flee the situation, my heart told me otherwise. He was speaking the truth. My shoulders loosened slightly, waiting for his next move.

"Do witches have mates?" He asked, lowering his hands so that they hung by his sides.

"What is a mate?" I replied with uncertainty.

"I guess you answered my question."

We stared back and forth at each other, unsure where to go from here. My body and the pull from my soul wanted me to run into his arms, crashing our lips together in a frenzy until he took me right there. Where were these thoughts even coming from? I had never had this type of attraction to a man before. Sure, I had seen men in town who were easy on the eyes, but none that I felt like I couldn't control myself around.

"Wolves, shifters...we have mates," he stated.

"You still haven't explained what a mate is," I said more harshly than intended.

He took a deep breath before answering.

"Mates are the other half of our souls. You know, the ying to my yang, the peanut butter to my jelly..."

What was he going on about? The more I thought it over, the more it made sense. My soul called to him as his to mine. Did that make us soul mates or kindred spirits? Soul mates? Was that even a thing?

"Watch," he said, stepping closer to me.

My breath hitched in apprehension with his movement. He moved more slowly, locking his eyes with me to show me I could trust him. He slipped his hand in mine.

"Do you feel that? The sparks?" he questioned.

I looked at our entwined fingers, feeling the sparks he described but not knowing if I was willing to accept their meaning. Was this all some kind of trick to lure me?

"It is a sign of our bond. Ever since I saw you by the creek yesterday, I haven't been able to free you from my mind. I waited outside your cabin, scared that you had left and I had lost my chance with you. When I saw your car drive back up the road, it was as if the moon goddess heard my prayers to bring you back to me."

My mind was swirling in thought.

"Wait...the moon goddess? You mean Selene?"

"Yes. She is our deity."

"She is ours as well."

Was she the one doing this? Did she bring me to him? Pair me with him? I needed to trust my gut, which told me to trust and go to him. I stepped closer, our bodies nearly flush together, and looked up at him.

"What does this mean?" I asked, my voice had become

breathy.

He leaned down and pressed his lips to mine. I tensed at first at the intimate contact, but within a moment, all of the anxiety that had stirred within me released, and I leaned into him. My body felt as if fireworks were exploding within it. I tried to pull closer to him, needing contact with his body as if he were my life-line. He wrapped his arms around me, engulfing me in his hold and furthering my desperate need for more contact. I gave in to my desire and deepened the kiss, parting my lips slightly. I felt his tongue push inside my mouth, meeting my own. I wrapped my arms around his shoulder, reveling in the comfort I felt from him.

His hands moved downwards until they passed the waist of my skirt, finding my ass and grabbing ahold of it. A small moan slipped from my mouth as his tongue still invaded it. This should be alarming to me. I had never even touched a man besides a rare handshake here or there. How did I even know what to do? I needed to stop thinking so much and just feel. As I released my last drop of control, we became frenzied, pulling each other closer. I let his hands push down at my waistband, dropping my skirt to the ground below. This should have felt wrong, but it didn't. For the first time in my life, this felt like the most right thing to be doing.

I allowed my hands to move across his back, noticing the defining muscles within. He grabbed my shirt's hem, lifted it over my head, and discarded it. I was not afraid of nudity, but this was the first time a man would see me. I felt his fingers fumble with the clasp of my bra before it dropped down my arms. I slung it away as if it had been blocking me from him. The last and final piece of my clothing soon slid down my legs, bringing me to the same state of undress that he stood before me in.

He gently laid me back into the grass. Fragrant flowers surrounded us, and the smell of earth permeated my nose. This was everything that I loved, and I was able to experience it upon giving up my virginity. His lips moved down my neck, sending the same sensation out as before. I lay beneath him, grabbing hold of every part I could grasp as his mouth worked its way to my breast, sucking it in. His hand roamed down my body, finding my entrance. I had never been touched like this before, at least not by anyone but myself.

At the coven, they taught that a woman's needs could be taken care of by herself. It was encouraged to appease your sexuality in the comfort of your own room. How I felt now far surpassed anything I could have done to myself. I felt his hardness press against my thigh, fueling my need for him. I reached down so that I could feel him. He was larger than I thought a man would be. My hand struggled to wrap around the full girth. My fingers held nothing compared to this. He moaned at the contact, and I began sliding my hand up and down his shaft. Feeling the need to have him inside of me, I guided him to me, teasing my entrance with the tip of him.

He pulled his head up, looking me in the eyes. "You need to know before we go any further. It is different from a wolf and his mate."

I paused for him to explain further.

"Once we start, I will have a hard time stopping. Everything in me pulls me to mate and mark you right now. If you are not ready for that, we should stop now."

I could tell he was struggling for control. Something I had already thrown out the window.

"I want it," I breathed out, almost in a fit.

"I will bite you," he said directly as if he had to get through the fine print.

"Then bite me," I urged, my need for him to be inside of me only growing as I ached between my legs.

"When I bite you, I will mark you, claiming you as mine."

"Get on with it!" I shouted, my voice heavy with lust.

The anticipation was driving me wild, a fitting thought for where and with whom I wanted to have sex with.

"The mark is forever. We will not be able to be apart."

The fleeting thought of my coven flashed through my mind, but once again, I gave in to what my body and soul were urging me to do and pushed all other thoughts away.

"Then take me forever," I said in a husky, disheveled tone.

"Are you sure?" his voice deepened, his own control slipping.

"How many times do I have to tell you to take me? I am yours forever. My body knows it, and I know it!" I nearly yelled at him.

His eyes darkened, and he smashed his lips to mine. I swore I could hear a growl come from him. He pushed himself into me, breaking my hymen and claiming my virginity. At first, it stung sharply, but only for a moment before the waves of pleasure took hold. I had never felt something as intense and satisfying as this in my twenty-two years. I gasped as he pulled back out, only to push back into me.

My body felt like it had a mind of its own, leading me to what to do, and I followed willingly. As he sucked in a breath near my shoulder, I turned my head to the side, giving him better access to do what he wished. My legs wrapped around his waist, wishing him deeper within me as my hands traveled across his back, grabbing hold with every thrust.

I could feel my muscles tighten as a climax grew. It felt like I would burst from the raw pleasure when I tightened around him. My breath caught in my throat as waves of pleasure coursed through my body like a rippling tide. I panted out a moan as my breath returned to me, and he slowed his movements, allowing me to release my taught body. He lifted one of my legs onto his shoulder, finding a new depth within me. I could feel my nails dig into his side as I fought a battle to keep myself grounded, one which I lost as I felt myself build quickly again.

"I'm going to mark you," he grunted between breaths.

"Yes," I moaned out.

The thought of him biting me sent another round of chills through me. I wanted it. I needed it. As I felt the same waves as before, I could feel him swell inside of me. He groaned as I felt a warmth spread into me. He kissed my shoulder, and his teeth grazed my skin, sending goosebumps across my skin. He began to apply pressure, building the intensity I already felt. When he punctured my skin, a euphoric blast exploded in me. It was as if we were floating in a pool of pleasure and desire. There was no pain, no thoughts—just us.

His movements stilled, and I could feel his tongue licking where he had bitten me. I focused on my breathing, willing it to return to normal. My body felt new and enlightened. It was as if a puzzle piece that had been missing had finally been placed, completing the work. His soft lips caressed mine, and I ran my hand through his hair, noting the silkiness. We looked into one another's eyes, and I felt I would get lost in them. Why would anyone deny themselves this? How could I ever stop?

9

Juniper

I played with the hair on Forest's chest, resting my head on his shoulder. The grass surrounding us had been matted down from our escapades. The first crickets of the evening began to play their song, which usually I could get lost in, but suddenly reminded me that I needed to return to the cabin before Heather and Meadow came looking for me. I sat up and looked for my clothing.

"I have to go," I said with a hint of panic, realizing my mistake.

It would take me past dark to walk back.

"Go where?" Forest asked with his own panic, nipping at his words.

"I have to get back to the cabin before the others come looking for me."

"I told you that we wouldn't be able to be apart. I don't know what it is like for a witch, but for a wolf, separating from your mate after you're first mated would be like burning hot pokers stabbing you in the chest."

I stopped and looked at him, concerned. He had said that...But I guess I hadn't thought it all the way through. Of course, I hadn't. I gave in to my body's primal desire to be with him. I could not deny our bond, but how would I explain this to the others? We were supposed to leave first thing in the morning. Even the thought of that brought an ache to my chest. Would I feel like he described? Would I feel like I was burning from the inside? I rid my mind of the thought.

"No matter what, I need to go talk to them. They will be worried if I don't return," I said, pushing myself up and redressing.

"Then I will go with you," he said in a determined voice as he followed me up.

"You can't. We are not supposed to bed a man unless it has been approved by the elders," my eyes shot at him with panic.

He looked at me with shock as he tried to wrap his mind around our customs.

"You have to get approval?" he said, stunned as if I just told him we grew two heads.

"Well, yeah...there are no men where I'm from," I tried to explain.

"How do you have children?" He asked.

"The women go to town and...you know," I shrugged as I pulled up my skirt.

He looked at me as if I spoke another language. I realized how foreign a concept it was to the rest of the world, but we were a matriarchal society and did what was needed to maintain our lifestyle and customs. Women lead and make all of the decisions. My Gran had told me that generations before her, when our families were still in the old country, they would have husbands and men, but they would often try to dominate the women, taking away their freedom and will. It was one of those men whose spite for being cast out sent the mob after them. They told the villages nearby how the women of our coven were seducing men to appease the devil. When they arrived in America, they vowed never to repeat the same mistake. I had never wanted to spend my life with a man, as I knew it was not in my cards, at least not until today. Not until I met him. I looked over his god-like features. Perhaps they were wrong. Maybe not all men are as domineering as those from the past.

"I will walk back with you there and wait outside," he said, returning the conversation to the task at hand.

I nodded at him, relief filling my body, knowing he would be close by. I still had to think of what I would say to Heather and Meadow once I returned. *Hey guys, I just went for a walk in the woods and got down and dirty with a wolf man I met. Oh, and by the way, we're mated and can never be separated.* They would think I had lost my mind. Did they even know about shifters? We were never taught about them. I would have to bring it up to Heather somehow and see if she knew anything. Forest took my hand as we started walking back. It felt natural but new. I looked down at our interlocked hands and felt a warmth spread in me. Everything about him felt right.

It was dark by the time we returned. I told Forest to wait outside, hidden from view. The only thing worse than returning with a man would be coming in with a man in all of his nude glory, as he had no clothes to dress in. Thinking of his body made me glance at it once more, bringing heat to my cheeks.

He pulled me against his taut-muscled body and kissed me lightly, "I will be right here. Just call if you need me."

I bit my lip as nerves shot through my chest from having to go in and face the music. I walked to the porch and slowly stepped up to the door. Just as I reached for the handle, the door flew open, and a worried Heather glanced me over.

"Where have you been? I told you to be back by dark. I did not mean when it was dark. I meant before it!" Her worry turned to anger.

"I'm sorry, Heather. I lost track of time, and it took me a while to get back."

Her stern face softened, "Let's not tell your Gran about this. It already took some convincing for her to allow you to come."

She pulled me inside, closing the door behind her. A lone plate of food sat at the table. They must have already eaten. I walked over, took my seat, and licked my lips. I had not had anything to eat since the brunch we were served at the meeting, and my stomach grumbled in protest. I watched Meadow walk down the stairs with a mug in her hand.

"And so she returns. Where did you wander off to? Looks like you went rolling in the dirt again."

I looked down at my skirt and realized what a mess I must have looked like. I ran my fingers through my curls, finding bits of grass tangled in them.

"Uh, yeah. I found a meadow and laid down. You know how I am," I said with a nervous laugh.

"Sure do," she joked, missing my nervous gestures.

She walked over to the stove and grabbed the tea kettle, filling it at the sink before returning it to the stove. Heather took a seat across from me and eyed me suspiciously. She always had a knack for detecting lies. One of the reasons Meadow could never get away with anything when we were kids. I hadn't necessarily lied. I just omitted some of the truth. I tried to remind myself of that as I scarfed down the herbed chicken breast in front of me. The silence in the room was stifling. It was an odd feeling with two of the closest women in my life. Meadow looked back and forth between us, obviously picking up on the unspoken tension. As the kettle whistled, she turned around, filling her mug.

"I think I'm going to go back to our room," she said over her shoulder, obviously wanting to avoid whatever storm was brewing.

"Okay," I said, trying to force confidence into my voice.

I felt Heather's heavy gaze on me as I watched Meadow return upstairs to our room.

Once the door clicked, Heather finally broke the silence, "What happened to you?"

"What do you mean?" I asked defensively.

She looked me over, "Something's different...You've changed somehow. Your whole aura is brighter. Does this have to do with whatever was pulling at you?"

I bit my lip, "Uh, yeah."

"What was it that called you?" she asked scrupulously.

I decided truth would be the best course. "I found this beautiful meadow. The entire time I was on my walk, there was something that kept drawing me deeper. It was like a song reaching for my soul," my voice softened as my memories revisited my story.

"And...?" There was a hardness in her tone as if saying that I needed to get to the point.

"Well, I found this wolf."

Her expression changed to one I could not decipher, but she stayed silent and waited for me to continue.

"I realized that he was what was calling to me. Not once was I fearful of this wild creature in front of me. It was a little alarming how calm I was, but it felt like I was supposed to meet him."

"Him? How did you know it was a boy?"

"What do you know of wolves?" I redirected the conversation, still not ready to admit to what I had seen and done.

She caulked an eyebrow, realizing what I was doing, "Wolves are wild animals in the canine family found throughout the northern hemisphere."

She was speaking far more factually and directly than usual. I could tell she knew more.

"Do you know of any special wolves?" I asked, prying her for more information.

She sighed heavily and looked down at her hands, twisting

them together. I could tell she knew about them. I wanted to ask why we were never taught about them, but I waited to see what she said. She looked back up at me, pursing her lips as if she were debating whether to tell me or not.

"There are many creatures in this world, Juniper. Just as we stay hidden, many others do as well. Humans are often unkind to things that they do not understand. I know of the type of wolf you are referring to. We had heard of the American wolves. They have several packs around the country, but we were unsure if they were the same kind-hearted beasts from the old country."

I leaned forward, "What do you mean?"

"A long time ago, creatures who could shift between man and wolf were our protectors. They watched over all women and children. Coming from a place where there were far more women and children than men, they stuck close to us. The one my grandmother was told about by her mother was called the Wulver. He lived in a cave nearby, and they would take care of him as a thank-you for his constant protection. When the mob came and burned down their homes, he fought them off long enough for the original six to escape. He was killed before he could save the others. If you are called to one of these creatures, perhaps there is a reason...What did you see?"

I let a breath out I had been holding, realizing it was time to confess about my situation with Forest.

"I approached the wolf. As I said, I felt no fear of it. In fact, I felt safe," I paused. "He...shifted into a man. I had never seen one so attractive as him."

She smiled at me, "I've heard they are good-looking."

My cheeks blushed, but I pushed on: "We talked. I was obviously surprised that an animal turned into a man in front of me, so it took me a minute to get over the shock. He knew I wasn't human, and something in me told me I could trust him, so I told him what I was."

Her lips pursed a little at my confession. One of the first things they taught us as children was never to reveal ourselves to someone outside of the coven, and I just broke that rule.

"How did he take it?"

"It didn't seem to worry him."

She nodded her head, "Good. It was a wonderful experience for you to have met one. Perhaps he was protecting you from something further in the woods. I'm just glad that you're back and safe."

She assumed that was the end, but it was only the beginning.

She started to stand from her chair, but I stopped her, "There's more..."

She looked at me as if trying to read my mind, but sat back down.

"He told me I was his mate," I blurted out.

"His, mate?"

"Yes. The other half of his soul. Once he confessed what that meant, it was like every puzzle piece of my life fell into place,"

My face lit up at the memory. She stared at me with a furrowed brow. I could see her mind spinning.

"Juniper, you cannot be his mate. They would never accept a man back at home; if he thinks you are his, he will not leave you be."

"He doesn't just think, Heather. He knows I am, as do I."

She ran her hand down her face, resting it on her cheek.

"I'm sorry, Juniper, but this is something that we will have to bring to the elders. I don't know what they will say about the situation. You can bring it up at the next coven meeting on Monday."

"No!" I nearly shouted.

I could have sworn I heard a low growl from outside at her recommendation. I peeked outside the window but only saw darkness. Could that have been him?

"Juniper," she started, pulling me from my thoughts again,

"you cannot stay here. The whole coven would fall into mayhem. I promised your Gran that I would bring you home. What will it mean if I return without you?"

"I..." Panic began to swell inside of me, but I pushed it down to try and remain level-headed. "Heather, every part of my being tells me that I need to stay with him."

"No," She said sternly, "I cannot approve of that. You at least need to come home and meet with the elders. We can leave tonight."

"I will not go," I said, standing from my chair.

"You must, and you will!"

We were shouting at each other at this point. Meadow opened the door from upstairs and peeked over the railing at us.

"What are you two arguing about?" she asked, concerned.

"Juniper here wants to stay," she said without looking away.

Her voice was filled with anger.

"Stay where?" Meadow asked as she moved to the top of the stairs.

"Vancouver," Heather replied in a heavy tone.

Meadow looked at me, stunned.

"Why would you stay here?" she asked softly as she walked down the stairs towards us.

"She met a man with whom she thinks she is in love," Heather accused.

"Our souls are bound. I cannot leave him."

"Wait, What? When did you meet a man? Was it in the city? At the office?" She looked out the window where a crack of lightning flashed from an incoming storm. "From your walk?"

"I'm sorry. To both of you. But I have to stay."

"Meadow," Heather called to her daughter. "Go pack the bags. We are leaving right now with Juniper."

"I said no," I argued back, meeting the same intense eye contact she had with me.

"Juniper, you are leaving me no other choice," she threatened.

What was she talking about? Would she call the elders? There was no phone here. Was she going to drag me out by my hair? My mind raced through all of the possibilities when I heard her begin to chant.

"*Dhòmhsa tha e mar fhiachaibh ort na tagraidhean agam a dhèanamh mar as toil leam.*"

"Stop!" I yelled as I noticed the air around me shimmer with the telltale signs of a spell being cast.

She never faltered.

"*Eisd rium, dèan mar a tha mi ag ràdh. Tilg mi mar sheirbhiseach dhomh thu gus an leig mi as thu.*"

I felt the control I had over myself lose its hold. My arms began to fall limp at my sides. I stood up as if being compelled to do so. Compelled...she had cast a compulsion spell on me. I was no longer in control of my body. I was a prisoner in my own mind. How could she do this to me? This was considered the dark arts, something banned within our coven. You could not take away a person's free will. I realized that I was trapped, unable to fight her off. I felt a tear prick at my eye, but it would not spill; even my own tears had been taken from me.

"Meadow, the bags!" Heather barked at her daughter, who stood frozen at the base of the stairwell.

I heard her footsteps run back upstairs. Heather ran her hands down her face and let out a whimper. I felt a rage inside me, one that did not feel like my own. What was it? Was this part of the bond I now shared? Could I be feeling Forest?

10

Forest

I paced back and forth behind the cabin, listening to Juniper's conversation with what I assumed was her family. I had mind-linked Oakley to bring me a set of clothes. I wanted to be prepared if she needed help. Listening in, it seemed they knew of werewolves; at least the older woman did, but they were unfamiliar with us. I was happy when she explained to Juniper how they were protectors of women and children. Perhaps they would have more approval of her staying with me if that had been their view. When she finally confessed our bond, the woman seemed exasperated, wanting her to return home to discuss it with the rest of her people, but Juniper put her foot down, telling her that she would not go. My chest puffed out in pride. She would do well in the pack.

Their argument soon turned to yelling as neither would concede to the other. A panic that I quickly recognized as Juniper's rose inside my chest, and I froze, keeping my ears to the house so that I would not miss anything. Everything had become silent, yet the panic was strong. The older woman told the younger one to get their bags. Were they leaving? Was the panic from her family leaving her? I crept to the side of the cabin to try and see inside the windows.

I couldn't see anything but heard them quickly moving around inside before the younger girl rushed out and loaded their bags in the trunk of their car. I would wait until they were gone before I went and checked on Juniper. I didn't want to add any more animosity to the situation. The older woman walked onto the porch and looked around as if searching for something. She was searching for me. I crouched further into the brush, making sure to stay perfectly still.

She looked back inside. "Juniper, get in the car."

What was she talking about? Juniper had already told her that she wouldn't leave. I heard the passion behind her testament to stay with me. I never heard them convince her. Juniper's panic that I felt in me grew, but I watched as she walked out the door. She looked strange. Not her carefree self. Where before, she moved naturally and smoothly as if gliding through the air. This seemed stiff and impersonal, as if she were a robot. Something wasn't right. Was she giving in and going? Was she leaving me? My own panic coursed through me, amplifying Juniper's. She slid into the back seat, staring forward. Not even a flinch or glance in my direction.

"Buckle up," the woman barked as she walked around the car.

"Mom, you can't do this," the younger one said to her in tears.

"I have to. It's the only way. We can't leave her here."

"She wants to stay. We should go back and talk to the elders ourselves."

"That would be the worst thing. I cannot return without her," the older woman chastised the other.

"Mom...please," the girl pleaded.

"Just get in the car, Meadow!" she shouted exhaustedly before climbing into the driver's seat.

The girl I now knew as Meadow climbed into the passenger seat and buckled in. The car began driving down the dark road. What should I do? I can't let her leave me.

Juniper? I mind-linked.

Shifters could speak telepathically to each other. We called it mind-linking. Juniper wasn't a shifter, but it was the only thing I could think of trying.

Juniper? I tried again.

Forest?

Yes, I replied, relieved. *It's me.*

Right. Now I'm imagining talking to you in my head, she said, unconvinced.

You're not imagining it. It's really me, I assured her.

How?

Wolves can speak telepathically.

I'm not a wolf.

I know, but you're my mate. I needed to try.

As they disappeared down the road, I began to follow, being sure to keep out of sight.

Are you alright? Why did you leave? I asked her, trying to hide the hurt I felt.

Heather, she's like an aunt to me. She's controlling me.

What do you mean? I angrily asked.

She cast a spell on me so that I would have to do everything she tells me to, she said fearfully.

You didn't want to leave? Hope resonated in my tone.

No! She shouted at me.

My heart filled with joy at her declaration to stay with me. I quickened my pace to catch up with them. I needed to stop them.

Oakley. I linked

Yes, Alpha.

*Gather a crew and meet me along the road leading away from the
Harper cabin. I'm following a car. You will need to find me, but stay in
stealth.*

Yes, Alpha.

I heard a distant howl. It was Oakley calling for reinforce-
ments. I needed to ensure Juniper's safety, and while I didn't want
to hurt her family, they were witches. My father warned me about
them when I was a child. Our pack had run into one here or there,
but they never were a threat, so we let them be. He told me they
were stronger than they appeared and never to underestimate
them if I were to get on their wrong side. I'm pretty sure taking
their niece away from them would put me on the wrong side of
them.

Forest. Juniper called out to me.

I'm here. I'm coming for you, I assured her.

Heather...she won't let you take me, she warned.

My determination pushed through, *I won't give her a choice.*

But I won't be able to go; her voice sounded mournful.

Why? I replied angrily.

It was not directed at her but towards her aunt. What she was
doing was wrong, and every warning my father had told me of the
witches resurfaced.

She has to release me. I'm in her control until she does.

I'll make her.

*You can't hurt her. I love them. They're my family, no matter how
wrong this is.*

I'll figure it out, I said, my frustration getting the better of me.

The dark, uneven roads and the rain that began to fall kept
them moving slowly. Luckily, this road would continue for a while,
giving my men the time they needed to group. The rest of my pack
would be able to catch up at this speed. Oakley would have called
the wolves' closet on patrol, saving the time from returning to the
pack house. I had only a little time to come up with a plan. The

car turned onto the main road leading down the mountain. It was asphalted, allowing them to speed up. Fortunately, the road continued to turn and twist for a while, keeping it at a pace I could easily match.

Oakley linked me, *We're coming. Where are you at?*

I'm heading south on the main road.

It was only a few minutes before I could hear them come up behind me. I never slowed in fear that I would lose the car. Oakley and the others joined me at my pace.

What's going on? Oakley linked me, including the others, in the connection.

Your Luna is in that car. A witch is controlling her, but we cannot harm them.

I could see Oakley's brownish-grey wolf look over at my revelation, but I could not get into more detail right now. We all needed to focus. The explanation would come later. They were nearing the end of the turns, where the road straightened out, and the speed limit increased. I was sure her Aunt would push the limit to get her away from here.

We need to stop them. I will cut them off. The rest of you surround the vehicle. Stay hidden until my signal. We need to put on a show of strength.

They each confirmed my directions as I sped up, cutting through the forest to where the road would cut back. I waited just past the turn so she had enough time to see me and stop before plowing through me. I stood in the middle of the road, ready to block the incoming car. As it rounded the corner, I saw the headlights dance across the trees and wet roadway. When they flashed in my eyes, the car slowed to a stop. Her Aunt, Heather, shakily stepped out of the driver's side, staying behind her door.

"You cannot have her. She does not belong here," her voice quivered.

I stood my ground. I could not communicate with her unless I shifted, and I knew I had a better shot of getting her back as my wolf. I took a step forward, showing her that I would not concede.

"I do not want to hurt you," I called out.

I took another step forward, again showing my protest.

"Please..." she begged.

Another step. She lifted her hands, and I let out a growl, baring my teeth at her. If she wanted a fight, I would not back down. With my signal of aggression, my men stepped forward, surrounding her vehicle and letting out their own growls of warning. Her head darted around, taking in the scope of her opponents. Her hands dropped back down. I could hear her erratic breathing as we stared at each other. I took another step forward, urging her to release Juniper.

She turned her face to the car, "Juniper, get out of the car."

I heard the click of a seat belt, and the back passenger door opened. The same robotic Juniper stepped out, standing perfectly still in the rain. The water flowing over her quickly weighed down her wild curls.

"You see, she does not go to you. She doesn't want to stay. Let us leave in peace."

Don't listen to her. Juniper linked me. *You have to tell her to release me.*

I took another step forward, ensuring she understood what she needed to do.

"Look for yourself. If she wanted to stay, she would run to you."

I realized that I needed to shift so that I could address her. I dropped my head and felt as my bones popped, reshaping into my other form. I stood tall, eyeing her down with conviction. Her face held a look of worry and surprise. I could see Meadow in the car with her hands over her mouth in shock. I knew my warriors would cover me if she chose to go on the offensive.

"Release her," I commanded.

"I did, don't you see. I told her to get out, yet still, she stands here, frozen with fear."

"Do not play games with me, witch. Release your hold on her. I do not enjoy your trickery."

Her mouth dropped open. She had not realized that I knew what she had done. She looked back at Juniper and then at me.

"If you want to go to him, then go."

Juniper walked stiffly to me, stopping directly in front of me. I could see her hidden in her eyes, but the person before me was not my Juniper. It pained me to see her this way, so detached and vacant.

I looked around her so that I could face her Aunt Heather.

"I said, release her. I will not ask again."

She took a deep breath and pursed her lips, looking like she was trying to find a way out. When I saw her shoulders slump, I knew she realized there was no other way. She lifted her hands, and the wolves began to growl. She stopped halfway, splaying her hands in a defensive gesture.

"I have to release her. It is the only way," she looked fearfully around her.

My nerves were shot. I didn't know if I could trust her. I looked at Juniper in her nearly vacant eyes.

Juniper, what should I do?

She must cast the spell to release me.

I looked back at the drenched woman, eyeing her suspiciously.

"Fine. But one wrong move and I will not hesitate to call for the attack."

She nodded her head nervously. She raised her hands, moving them in a circular motion.

"*Bidh mi a 'leigeil a-mach do cheangal. Is i do thoil fhèin.*"

Juniper took a sharp breath in, and her body loosened. The light in her eyes returned. I ran my hand down her cheek, inspecting her. She looked down at my nude body, and her cheeks reddened. She whipped around and faced her aunt, yet stood in front of me as if she were blocking the sight of me from her family.

"I cannot believe you. You were one person I always thought I could trust, and you broke it. You broke everything I ever thought of you," Juniper sneered through gritted teeth.

"Juniper, please. This is not how to do this. Come back with us and plead your case to the elders. I will drive you back once they approve."

"This is my life and my choice! Our souls are bound. I cannot leave. I am safe here. He is safe."

"I cannot leave you," her aunt cried.

Juniper's expression softened, and she walked to her and held onto her hands.

"You must. Now go."

She turned back around and walked back to me. She took my hand and pulled me to the side, opening the road. Her aunt hesitated for a moment as she watched us. Remembering my father's warning, I was still on edge, waiting for the woman's next move. She looked at Juniperone last time before climbing back into the car. Pressing on the gas, her eyes pleaded with Juniper as she drove by. Once they turned the next corner and the sound of their engine faded, I called out to my men.

"Return home. We will follow shortly."

The wolves around us turned to the forest and raced back in, disappearing into the darkness. Juniper looked up at me through her long eyelashes. I reached out and held her waist, sparks flooding my body. I could see tears masked behind the raindrops that littered her face.

"It takes a strong person to stand up for themselves," I whispered to her.

She wiped her face and gave a strained smile. I could feel the hurt inside of her. Betrayal never comes by lightly.

"Thank you for coming for me," she said softly.

"I will always come for you."

She stepped into my body, wrapping her hands around me. I returned the gesture, resting my chin on her head before kissing it, savoring her scent. I meant what I had said. Nothing could keep me from her now.

11

Forest

"Before we go anywhere, I need to do something," Juniper stopped me as I began to lead her to the forest.

I looked at her questioningly. She ran her hands down her face and pushed them to the ground as if pushing the air with them. I sensed an energy move along her. Then, in a mesmerizing voice, she began to chant.

"*Chan fhaighear mi tuilleadh, tha mi neo-fhaicsinneach don treas sùil. Air chall don t-saoghal, tha mi a' co-dhùnadh cuin a lorgar mi*"

She looked up at me with a smile, "I'm ready."

"What was that?"

"I just wanted to be sure they don't follow me."

"I would sense them if they tried."

"Not if they used a tracking spell. They could return tomorrow, next week, or even in a month. I never thought they would do something like a compulsion spell on me," her voice turned somber. "I don't want to take any chances."

It made sense. I would have to get used to her being a witch and all that entailed. I should have considered the methods they could use to track us down, but this was all mostly new. I had never personally interacted with witches before. Some packs used their services, but we never did. I wondered what else she could do. I decided to leave these thoughts for later when we weren't standing on the side of the road.

It had taken me a few minutes to convince her to ride my wolf's back to the pack house. She was not confident that she would stay on. She forgot how large my wolf was, and her petite 5'2" frame was nothing for me. It felt like heaven winding through the trees. The joy I felt from her closeness and the bond, paired with the satisfaction of being between her legs, could not be beaten. Even the rain could not deter the happiness I felt at that moment.

When we reached the edge of the village, I slowed, allowing her to climb off of me so we could walk together. After I shifted back, I stopped at one of the clothes boxes attached to a tree to grab a pair of sweats from inside. I slipped them on before continuing. The flickering lights of craftsman-style homes danced as we walked past.

"What is this place?" She asked, looking around.

"This is the West Moon Pack. Our home."

"Is everyone here...like you?"

I let out a laugh. "You mean wolves? Yes. This is our village. It's disguised as just another town. We have a small main street with stores and a diner, but everyone who lives here and works here is part of our pack."

"How do you keep the humans out?"

"The road that comes in stops here, so we don't get people just passing through. And it's out of the way of any other city. On the odd occasion that some human or tourist decides to explore, we have patrols that watch the road. They send a signal out to notify everyone. Sometimes they shop our stores and will eat here, but without a place to stay, they usually leave within an hour or two."

Her face was filled with wonder as she looked around.

"Where do you live?"

"You mean we. My home is yours now."

She smiled up at me.

"Okay, where is our house?" She entertained me.

"I live at the pack house."

"What's that?"

"Think of it as the headquarters," I attempted to explain.

"Do a lot of people live there?"

"No. Just my Beta Oakland and my Gamma August."

What is a Beta and a Gamma?"

"They are my second and third."

"Does every home have a Beta and Gamma?"

I found her questions adorable. She had no clue about pack dynamics, something I was sure she would pick up quickly, and I was excited to teach her.

"No. Just me."

"Why just you?"

"I'm the Alpha."

She stopped and looked at me. "What do you mean?"

"I lead the pack."

Her mouth dropped slightly. "So you're in charge, like, of everyone here?"

I laughed at her surprise, "Yes."

"I...Wait, what does that make me? I'm not in charge, am I?"

"You're their Luna. Their female leader," I said proudly.

"Hold up." She said, holding up her hands and staring at me in disbelief. "I'm their female leader? Like...I'm in charge, too?"

"Yes." I couldn't help the grin on my face as she processed the information. "A Luna helps lead alongside the Alpha. She is the heart of the pack."

"I-I don't know if I can do that. I'm not even a wolf. How could I help lead them if I'm not one of them?" Uncertainty spread across her face.

I pulled her closer, wrapping my arms around her. "After everything I've seen today, there is no doubt you can."

She bit her lip in nervousness.

"Come on, I want to show you where you live now."

I held her hand in mine and walked the rest of the way to the pack house. It was one of the only stone buildings in the entire village, besides some shops on the main street. It looked like a mansion to anyone else, standing tall at the end of a side street. A large stone fountain out front with wolves carved into its features. The circular drive wrapped around the feature, adding to its grandeur. The house rose three stories tall with large windows and carved corner accents. A large wooden double door stood at the center.

I watched Juniper's head move around as we entered, taking in the intricate details. The white granite floors contrasted with the dark mahogany walls. Two large staircases wrapped around either side, leading to the second floor.

"This door in front of us takes you to the offices. Each of the high-ranked wolves has one." I could see the confusion on her face, so I elaborated, "Oakley, August, and myself."

She nodded her head.

"To the right are the dining room and kitchen, and to the left are the sitting rooms. There is also a library back that way." I pointed to the far left corner. "They are all connected in a large loop, so finding your way around is easy."

I led her up the stairs and wrapped around the second set directly above the first.

"Oakley and August's apartments are on this floor," I said before ascending to the third floor.

Another set of double doors was centered against the wall at the top of the stairs. I opened one side and gestured her in.

"And this is our apartment."

We walked into the large living room, which was furnished with a sizable sectional sofa to the right. My 70" television was mounted to the wall above a cabinet with built-in bookshelves flanking it on either side. To the left was a small kitchen with modern black cabinetry and a large island with stools lining one side. A sleek, natural wood table sat beside it, closest to the entry.

"This is beautiful," she said, walking further into the space.

"I'm glad you like it."

I gave her a moment to look around.

"I have to go talk to the others. I'm sure they are wondering about what happened tonight. The master bedroom is through the last doors in the hallway. Make yourself at home, and I will return shortly."

I walked up and kissed her, savoring every second of it before turning back the way we had come. The last thing I wanted to do was leave her right now, but I knew I owed the others an explanation. I went to my office and found Oakley and August sitting on the leather sofa against the wall. Just where I expected them to be. They stood when I walked into the room.

"Congratulations, man," Oakley said, patting me on the back. "How did you find her, and what the hell was that all about?"

I sat down on one of the matching armchairs next to them.

"I found her yesterday while I patrolled the south border. It was like watching a nymph dipping her toes in the water, calling out to me."

"Why didn't you bring her back then?"

"Honestly," I said, running my hands through my hair. "I wasn't positive she was."

I didn't want to admit my hesitation to claim her then. I had caught the scent of lavender and sage and followed it, finding her.

When I saw her resting on a boulder, leaning back on her arms and pushing her breasts to the sky, I wanted to take her right there, but her scent was not that of a wolf. Wolves only mated with wolves. There were a few rare occasions when one would choose a human as a mate, but true mates were always the same as us.

"How could you not know?"

I hesitated to answer, though I knew it had to come out. "She's not a wolf."

"What?" They both yelled at the same time.

"How is that possible?" Oakley asked.

"I don't know. All of last night, my wolf was restless and pushed me to find her again. When I saw her today, there was no mistaking it."

"How did she get mixed up with the witches? She seemed close to them," August asked, taking a drink of his bourbon.

"They're her family."

"You're telling me you mated with a witch?" Oakley said as if he was trying to convince himself. "How do you know they didn't put some spell on you to make you think she was your mate? They're witches!"

"That's enough," I growled at his insult to Juniper. "I know that there is no spell."

"How can you be sure?"

"I just know. Plus, we can mind link."

"That can't be. Only shifters can link," August spoke more levelly.

"I don't know what to tell you. It's new territory for me, too. But deep inside me, I know who she is to me."

"Okay. Well, how are we going to handle this? I'm not sure everyone will accept her as their Luna since she's not a wolf," Oakley said, leaning back in his seat.

"Then they can leave. The Moon Goddess gave her to me, and I will not turn her away," I said with determination.

"Alright, alright. I was just stating the obvious."

"You can be happy for me and accept your Luna or fuck off with anyone else who fights her claim," I stared at him.

He put his hand up defensively, "I do accept her. I'm happy for you both. It's just...unheard of."

I poured myself a bourbon from the bottle on the table and sat back in my chair.

"Can you at least elaborate on what went down tonight?"

"Let's just say her family is not accepting our mating either," I grunted.

"Hey, Forest, listen. I am accepting of her. It's my job as your Beta to watch your back. I just needed to be sure," Oakley said, leaning his elbows on his legs.

The tension was thick in the room.

"Do you think we need to worry about her family?" August chimed in.

"I don't know. We should send a few extra patrols out just in case."

"Sure thing, boss," Oakley returned to his relaxed position on the sofa.

I stared at both of them, polishing off my drink before standing.

"We can talk more about this tomorrow. I want to get back to her."

"Just one more thing..." Oakley added.

"What?" I was getting aggravated.

"What are you going to do about Sienna?"

Fuck. I forgot about Sienna. She had been a good bed warmer for the last year or so, but I had never thought of her as anything more. She was easy and available. I knew she wanted me to take her as a mate, but I kept her around against my better judgment. Now, she's a complication. She liked the status of being with me and everything that it got her, but she would have to accept my bond, just like everyone else.

"You can let her know tomorrow."

"She will already know. You just announced to a whole herd of warriors that you found your mate. Pair that with the fact that your new Luna isn't even a wolf; Sienna is going to throw a fit."

"He's right," August added. "She should be told tonight. And we should put a tail on her to ensure she doesn't try anything."

"She knows her place. It would be a death sentence to attack her Luna. But Oakley, go inform her tonight."

"Will do."

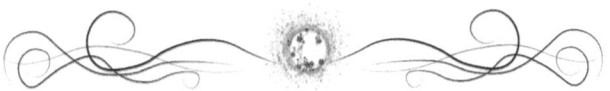

12

Juniper

After Forest left, I wasn't sure what to do. He said this was our home, but it was still new. Was I allowed to look around? I looked down at my drenched clothing and felt a shiver. I could take a shower and warm up. I walked down the hall, noting several closed doors. I would have to ask him about them when he gets back. I turned the knob to the door at the end of the hall, opening it up to a large white room with a massive bed at the center, sitting between two large windows. A cabinet sat at the foot, but I saw no doors. Strange...

A small sitting area was on the opposite wall, and several doors across the room. I walked over to the closest one and opened it. Thankfully, I found the bathroom on my first try. It was bigger than my bedroom back at the coven, with double sinks and a built-in vanity table between them. White marble with grey veins sat on top of the natural wood cabinets. Centered beneath the large picture window stood a clawfoot tub with gold legs. A shower with a glass door that could fit at least ten people was in the corner.

I walked over and inspected the knobs on the wall inside. There were so many! I tried the first one and found nothing happened. When I turned the second, the water shot on. It seemed to control the pressure. The more I turned it, the harder the water flowed. I tested the temperature, finding it cold. Playing with each knob, I discovered that one controlled the temperature while the others seemed to turn on jets that ran down the wall. I finally figured out the setting I wanted before removing my clothes and stepping in.

The water felt amazing after the day I had just had. I let the jets massage the aching muscles down my back. I inspected the bottles on a recessed shelf and found shampoo and conditioner. I noticed that there were two sets. One was simple with almost no scent, while the other had a strong floral scent that nearly made my eyes water. Why would he have such fragrant shampoo? I grabbed the plain one and lathered it through my hair. Finishing up with the conditioner, I ran my fingers through my hair, pulling out the tangles.

For how much I wanted to stay in, I wanted to be done by the time he returned, so I reluctantly turned the water off and stepped out, grabbing a towel from the shelves nearby and wrapping it around me. I dried myself off and looked in the mirror. I could finally see what Heather had been talking about. My face looked brighter. Each part of my body looked like it had gained some color, even my hair, which I didn't think was possible. I grabbed a second towel and wrapped my hair up in it.

I looked down at the soggy clothes piled on the floor, and I remembered my bag, which was left in the trunk of the car. How could I forget to grab it? I had nothing. I took a deep breath and decided that I would have to figure something else out. I hoped he would be alright if I borrowed something from him.

I walked back into the bedroom and went to the next door. It opened to a grand closet almost the same size as the bathroom. A white settee was sitting against the back wall with floor-to-ceiling mirrors. I noticed that the shelves were bare. Maybe he didn't have many clothes? I mean, after all, every time I've seen him, he was naked. I decided to check some of the drawers. The first one was empty. When I opened the second, it was full of panties and bras. Why would he have these? Did he remember that I had no clothes and had some brought over? That made no sense. When would he have had time? I picked up one of the bras, holding it up to my chest. There was no way I would fit into this. I may be small-framed, but my bosom was not lacking.

It suddenly occurred to me that these were not for me at all. These were another woman's. Had I slept with a taken man? He had never given me a clue that he was unavailable. Maybe I missed something? It's not like I was well-versed in men. In fact, I have talked to very few in my lifetime. The only interaction I had had was talking to a few men in town when we would go to the movies or shopping. Mr. Jones was the longest interaction I had with a man until I met Forest.

Dammit. I needed to get out of here. Heather was right. I should have left. I walked back out, returned to the bathroom, and grabbed the heap of soggy clothing off the floor. I took them to the sink and rang them out as best I could. I dropped the towel and attempted to pull my skirt up. It clung to my legs with its icy grasp. I would forgo the underwear until they dried out more. I pulled my shirt over my head. It, too, clung to me, accentuating my breasts beneath it. It would have to do.

I peeked out of the bedroom, listening for Forest before tiptoeing down the hall. The last thing that I needed was a confrontation. My heart would not be able to handle it. Luckily for me, he had yet to return. I opened the apartment door, again listening for any signs of others. If I could slip out of here, maybe

I could make my way into the city and find a way to call the coven.

I reached the second floor before I heard someone walking up from the first. I pinned myself behind a corner that led to another door, holding my breath not to give myself away. A tall, blonde-haired man walked to the door opposite where I was hidden and entered. That must be either his Beta or Gamma. If he were here, I assumed it was only a matter of time before the others followed, including Forest. Panicking, I remembered the spell Meadow, and I used to cast when we snuck out as kids.

"*Thig còmhla rium leis na ballachan agus na speuran. Dèan mi neo-fhaicsinneach don t-sùil.*" I whispered, running my hands down my body.

I lifted my hand and inspected it. Nothing could be seen. Invisibility spells could be useful, especially when you need to go unnoticed. I walked carefully down the steps and to the front door. My chest ached at the thought of leaving, but I could not stay. I would not be the other woman to a man. One that every part of me claimed as my own. Even the thought of sharing him felt like a dagger stabbing into my gut. I grabbed hold of the handle right as I heard footsteps coming from my right. I froze and held my breath, not wanting to give myself away.

Forest carried a tray with two plates of food in his hands. He stopped when he came into the room and looked around. Could he feel me like I could him? Goosebumps littered my skin the closer he came.

"Forest," a voice suddenly called from where he told me his offices were.

He turned to look at the brunette man who approached him.

"I know you feel confident that she will not do anything, but I really feel like we should tail her. She won't like having her status taken away."

"If you feel that strongly, August, then set something up. Has Oakley gone to tell her yet?"

"I don't think so."

"Argh. Make sure that he does. And tell him to let me know what her reaction is. I know it won't be good, but maybe he can gauge if she will try something."

"Yes, Alpha."

They began walking up the stairs together.

"How many times do I have to tell you to call me Forest when it's just us?"

"It just doesn't feel right."

They turned the corner at the top, and I took advantage of the moment to quietly open the door and slip out. I looked around, unfamiliar with the area. The rain had lightened but still held a steady rhythm. Hopefully, it would help me escape. I quickly made my way back the way we had come. My best bet would be to hide in the forest, trying to find my way back to the cabin I stayed at with Heather and Meadow. I was pretty sure that I could find my way into the city from there, though it would take me a day or two to walk it.

Due to the rain, very few people were out. I felt an intense pain of grief in my chest. Was it my own? With no one in sight and the rain picking back up, I ran to the forest, disappearing into its dark hold.

13

Forest

After talking with Oakley and August, I decided to get Juniper and me some food. She had been through a lot tonight, and I wanted to make her feel at home. I walked into the kitchen and dug through the fridge. We had several pack members who staffed the pack house during the day, one of whom was an amazing cook. She always stocked a few things in case we got hungry after she had gone home.

I pulled out a container of lasagna and heated it in the microwave. I felt sadness run through me. Juniper must still be sad about her family. Hopefully, this will help. I divided the food up and placed it on two plates. I grabbed a tray from the pantry and put the plates on it. When I stepped into the foyer, Juniper's scent filled my nose. It was so strong it was as if she were right there with me. I felt the bond tug at me toward the door. It seemed too strong to be from when we had come in. I took a step toward the door to investigate.

"Forest," August called from the other hallway. "I know you

feel confident that she will not do anything, but I really feel like we should tail her. She won't like having her status taken away."

I was annoyed that he was keeping me from my mate but also happy that he was taking his duty so seriously. As Gamma, he was in charge of Juniper's protection, among numerous other responsibilities.

"If you feel that strongly, August, then set something up. Has Oakley gone to tell her yet?"

"I don't think so."

Oakley was getting on my nerves. I couldn't believe the accusations he had made about Juniper. She was his Luna, and he needed to respect that. I get that it's not the norm, but challenging the validity of our bond took it a step too far. After he had asked me, I searched deep inside myself for any doubt, finding none. I didn't need to be second-guessing her. She was mine. Every ounce of me knew it with certainty.

"Argh. Make sure that he does. And tell him to let me know what her reaction is. I know it won't be good, but maybe he can gauge if she will try something."

"Yes, Alpha."

"How many times do I have to tell you to call me Forest when it's just us?"

"It just doesn't feel right."

I laughed at him as he knocked on Oakley's door. I stopped atop the steps near my door to hear what they said.

"What's up, August?" Oakley asked as he answered his door.

"You need to go talk to Sienna."

"Man, she is going to lose her shit," he grunted.

"I know, but you still have to do it."

"Do you think she will be at her house?"

"There, or you could try the diner. You know she hates cooking."

"She'd probably poison herself if she ate her food," Oakley's mischievous voice said.

They both laughed.

"You'd better go now. He was asking if you had left yet."

"Alright...Just has to be fucking raining tonight."

"Get it done quickly so you can return to your spank bank."

"That's not what I was doing."

"Sure," August teased.

Satisfied, I entered my apartment and set the food on the table.

"Juniper?" I called out.

She didn't answer. I walked down the hall and into our bedroom. The bathroom door was cracked open, and light showed through. I grinned at the prospect of seeing her body. When I opened the door, I found the room empty. Several towels were on the floor, and the shower walls were wet. She had taken a shower. I'm glad she did as I told her to make herself at home. I wished that I had stayed to get her settled in before going down to talk to the others. I realized how cold she must have been from the rain. It didn't affect us much since our bodies ran so warm.

I noticed the door to the spare closet I had saved for my mate ajar. I opened it, again finding it empty. Just as I turned to leave, I noticed something sticking out of one of the drawers. Why would anything be in here? I had told the maids to leave it empty, only wanting to fill it with clothes for my Luna, for my Juniper. I walked over, pulling it out. A thin, black-laced bra dangled on my finger. It reeked of Sienna. She must have snuck clothes in here when I wasn't looking.

Panic set in. Did Juniper find this?

"Juniper?" I called loudly, only to be met with silence.

I ran through each room of my apartment, finding them empty. I was filled with grief. What must have gone through her head, finding another woman's bra in what she would assume to be my closet? Is that why her scent was so strong downstairs? Had she left?

Oakley, August...

Yes, Alpha, August immediately answered.

Search the house. Juniper is missing!

Where would she have gone? Oakley asked.

I don't know. I caught her scent earlier near the door. Send the warriors out to look for her.

Yes, Alpha, they both said in unison.

I ran down the stairs and out the front door into a heavy storm. With all the rain, there would have been no way to track her out here, and her scent trail would have been quickly washed away.

Juniper? I called her through our mind link. *Please answer me.*

Just let me go, Forest. I don't want to be someone's sidepiece.

You're not. You are the only one for me, I pleaded.

Knowing that she had indeed left, I raced to the forest, shifting into my wolf, shredding the clothes I had on to go in search of her. She would most likely try to return to the only landmark she had out here, the Harper Cabin. I took off towards it, going quickly but not too fast that I would miss her.

Juniper, did you hear me? You are the only one I want.

I cursed internally at Sienna, sneaking her stuff in. She had already been trying to take the place of Luna, and I had been too complacent to realize it. I should have stopped it when she left some toiletries in the bathroom. She told me I could at least allow her that since she slept over so much. August and Oakley warned me about her, but she seemed like a good fix for the emptiness I felt without a mate. Though I was not too old at twenty-six, Alphas usually found their Lunas younger. It was like the Moon Goddess bringing balance early on to a pack with their level heads.

After my father had died two years ago at the hands of a human hunter who had slipped past our eastern border, I took over suddenly. He had trained and prepared me, but the sudden thrust to power took me a few months to gain footing. The whole first year, I felt immense pressure to live up to what my father had always thought I could be. Sienna had made herself available. Her tall, slender figure with shoulder-length blonde hair and bronzed skin was a nice place to vent my frustrations. I had always let her know that we were not exclusive. I even had a fling with a few other women around the pack, wanting her to realize that she was not the one for me, but I gave in to the ease of having one person who came whenever I called. I let the simplicity of her attachment push past boundaries that should never have been crossed.

I neared the cabin, looking for any trace of her. I didn't think I had missed her, but just fifty yards or so in this weather would have hidden her from my senses. I shifted and ran up the porch, trying the door and finding it locked.

Juniper, where are you?

She didn't answer me.

Come on, Juniper. You can get lost out here. My desperation was evident as I pleaded to her.

The cabin was around ten kilometers away from the village through dense forest that wrapped around the mountain. It would be easy for someone who does not know the area to get lost or turned around. The towering trees blocked any distinguishable landmarks from the ground. As wolves, we knew our territory. We'd grown up here, memorizing every rock, stream, and fallen log. Besides that, we had an inherent knack for direction.

Oakley, have a warrior scout out the cabin in case she returns there.

Yes, Alpha.

I turned back to the woods and began combing the area. I would work my way back to the village, checking for her hiding along the way. Perhaps she found a place to shelter until the storm passed. It would be the smart thing to do.

14

Juniper

My water-logged clothing felt glued to my skin, impeding my movements as I climbed over a fallen tree. Everything was soaking wet and had long become slippery, making my travels slow and grueling. I didn't remember the forest being so dense on the way to Forest's pack, though I was not exactly paying attention as I rode on the back of his massive wolf. All I had thought of was what the coven would have felt seeing me riding a wolf through the woods.

Juniper, where are you? Forest linked me again. *Come on, Juniper. You can get lost out here.*

I couldn't answer him, not if I wanted to actually leave. After our last conversation, my chest tightened. He said I was the only one for him, yet I found undeniable evidence contradicting that statement. I just needed to keep going. Eventually, I would find my way back. I just needed to get through the night.

I pushed through the sea of ferns and brush that stood in my way, feeling my skirt tear at the bottom. I looked down to find a large piece of fabric now dragging on the ground. Dammit. I reached down and tore it the rest of the way off, discarding it on the ground. I hated to think what I would look like after this. I could feel the slight sting from all the scratches I had acquired. My clothing was becoming more torn and muddied the farther I walked. By the time I actually found the city, everyone would mistake me for some crazy transient. I had nothing to prove who I was. Heather had my passport and driver's license, the only pieces of identification I owned.

Though we did not leave the coven much, the elders always insisted that we have all the proper documentation needed if we ever had to flee the settlement. It was the same reason we were taught to drive cars. Not so much so that we can drive around, but as a means to escape should the need arise. I was thankful for it when we heard of the trip to Vancouver. Without them, we would not have been able to come on such short notice. I would figure it all out once I found my way there.

Soon, I was faced with a small cliff in front of me. We definitely had not come this way. I ran my hands down my face, clearing the water that flowed down it. I could not see if it shortened in one direction or the other. I decided to go left, thinking that it would be the direction that the city would be. With any luck, I could at least find a road.

Juniper, Forest called to me in my mind. *I know you're listening. I'm sorry. I should have waited for you. I became restless waiting to find you and did not make smart decisions. There were other women in my life, but nothing serious.*

I scoffed at his confession. Having clothes and even her shampoo, all seemed pretty serious to me. I had come to realize as I fought my way through the overgrowth that the floral shampoo he had in his shower must have been this other woman's. It was as if she lived there or at least stayed there often. When was the last time she had been there? Was it last night after I sensed him near the creek? Lies...it's what we were always warned about with men back home. They would say anything to take advantage of you.

You are my mate, Juniper! The other half of my soul. I cannot live without you. Please let me at least explain things to you.

Perhaps I should. It was never good to jump to conclusions. Anger filled me as I remembered the tiny lace bra that I held in my hands. It was so sexy, so alluring. I owned nothing of the sort. Most of the time, I didn't even wear a bra, finding it constricting. The few I had were soft, white cotton. We had always gone for ease and comfort. If he was attracted to a woman who wears stuff like that, then I was definitely not for him. My chest tightened again at my train of thought. Along with my surge of emotions, I could feel other emotions that were not my own. Grief and sadness...regret and anger. They were what I felt but separate from my own in a way as if I could sense someone else's. I tripped over a stick on the ground, landing hard on my knees. I needed to block these foreign emotions out so that they would not distract me. I needed to keep my wits about me in this environment. I rubbed my sore knees, finding a little blood on my hands. I looked down at them and saw I had given myself a good cut across one from another branch I had landed on, adding another hole to my skirt.

Are you okay? Forest asked, concerned.

How did he know something was wrong? Was he close? I looked around for any signs of him, but only faced the near-black forest and the deafening sound of the rain. I waited for a lightning strike, giving me the slightest glimpse of my surroundings. I saw no one else out in this chaotic scene. The rain, which helped me, also hindered me. It helped hide any trail I left behind, but it made it nearly unmanageable to navigate the dense woods.

I kept my eyes alert as I started walking again, following the cliffside. The wind picked up, sending rain into my face. I held a hand over my eyes to shield them from the onslaught of water. Perhaps I should wait out the worst of it before continuing on. I could barely see where I was going, and the water pelting my face had nearly blinded me. I decided that I would go until I found someplace safe to hunker down for an hour or two.

Answer me, Juniper. I can't lose you.

The pain in his voice, which was overwhelmed with fear, made me falter in my steps. This all seemed wrong. What was I doing? Was I just being some overdramatic girl throwing a fit? The jealousy of thinking he was currently with another woman made me flee. He said the other women he had been with were not serious, even though having their stuff in his closet seemed the contrary. Afraid I was overreacting, I decided that I should at least hear him out.

Forest.

Juniper, thank the goddess. Are you okay?

I don't know where I am, I told him.

I'll find you. What do you see?

Before I tell you, I need to know about the woman's personal belongings in your room. That seems more than the 'non-serious' relationship you claim it to be.

I had no idea that she had left stuff there. She was just a fling. From day one, I told her we would never become something more. I was waiting for you.

Obviously not waiting, I chastised.

You're right. I didn't wait. Not in that way. But my heart has always only been meant for you. I would choose you over anyone else every time. We are meant to be with each other.

I will agree to come back on one condition: If I find that you are not faithful to me or that you are lying, you will drive me to the city and let me go, I stated my demands.

I felt proud of myself. If he agreed, then we would be able to discuss things further, allowing me to make a conscious decision based on facts rather than being fueled by emotion. If I did decide to leave, I would not be lost in the forest in a raging storm trying to fight my way out.

I agree, but promise that you will hear me out before deciding.

Okay, I promise.

From the moment we agreed to terms to resolve our situation, I felt an immediate relief wash over me.

I'm near a cliff. I've been following it for a while.

I think I know where you are. I'm on my way.

I smiled at his determination to get to me. I turned around and decided to go back the way I had come. I stayed close to the cliff when I suddenly tripped on a rock jutting out of the ground. It happened so fast that I could not get my hands up fast enough to catch myself. I felt my head slam onto a rock, making my vision spin. I could faintly hear Forest yelling my name in my head, but the blackness of unconsciousness quickly consumed me.

Forest

I FELT immense relief that Juniper would allow me to explain everything. I hated the stipulation that I would let her leave if I could not convince her of my commitment to her, but at least I wouldn't have to worry about her out here. I had been so scared she would get hurt or, worse, killed. The forest had many hidden dangers, especially with all of this rain. The ground could easily give way beneath her, tossing her down a hill, or she could cross paths with a wild animal like a bear.

When she told me that she was near a cliff, I could think of a few options, but the fact that she had been walking along it for a while made me believe she was north of the cabin near the ridge. As I raced in her direction, I could feel the pull in me. How had I overlooked the invisible tether between us? I could always feel which way she was. I would have found her if I had been more in tune with my senses rather than blindly scouring the forest in a panic. I came to a sudden halt at a sharp pain in my head. It was Juniper's pain. She was hurt.

Juniper! Juniper! I yelled over and over at her.

She wasn't responding. I needed to get to her fast. I pushed myself harder, moving as fast as I could.

She is near a cliff. Send the warriors to the ridge and any other cliff you can think of. She's hurt. I shot through the link to Oakley and August.

I heard them reply, but tuned them out as I focused on our bond. I could feel her near as I approached the ridge. She never said whether she was above or at the bottom of the cliff. I jumped up the steep rocks to the top, nearly ten meters up. I figured that I would be able to look over both from this angle. I slowed my pacing, being sure not to miss her. Water was running down the edges of the rock and dirt. Landslides had caused the drop to my right, which fueled my worry for her. With all of this rain, it had the potential to slide again.

I nervously peeked over the side a few times, not wanting to push the integrity of the edge. I spotted her limp form collapsed a few meters away from me, lying at the base of the cliff. I looked for a way to climb down, but no large rocks were sticking out that I could use. I ran past her to where I knew of a recent rock slide and raced down the small ravine it had left. When I approached her, I could smell her blood in the air. Even with the rain, you could not cover that smell. She must have bled a good amount for it to be so strong. I shifted and gently rolled her over, inspecting her face. Blood poured down from a gash just above her temple. A blood-covered rock lay jutting from the earth to the side of her. She must have tripped. I scooped her up in my arms and began running back to the pack.

I found her. Call the doctor to the clinic. She hit her head, I linked Oakley.

Yes, Alpha.

I would let him worry about calling in the search party. Right now, I just need to get her to the clinic. The village was still four kilometers away, and running in my human form slowed me. I glanced down at her pale face. Her lips were blue from the cold. I held her tighter to try and warm her with my body heat. I inspected her injury as I ran. Even with the rain helping to wash the blood away, fresh blood flowed freely from the wound. She was losing too much. I stopped and gently laid her down, tearing the bottom of her shirt to wrap around her head to slow the blood loss. I tied the strip of fabric in place before picking her back up. I was determined to get her back as fast as possible.

It felt like an eternity before we returned to the village. Even though it was a late hour, I could see people looking out of their windows from all the commotion. I noticed them watching me run with Juniper in my arms through the buildings. The clinic was at the end of the main street. The lights were already on inside, signaling that Oakley was able to get the doctor over there quickly. I pushed the door open with my foot.

"Back here, Alpha," Dr. Stone called from the back room.

I brought her in and laid her unconscious body on the table in front of him. He stepped forward to examine her, and I let out a growl. My wolf stirred inside me over my injured mate. He was highly protective right now and seemed to think of the doctor as a threat. Oakley's warning that others might not take too kindly to a witch brought more anxiety to me. Would he accept her for what she was?

He looked up at me, surprised, before lowering his head, appeasing my wolf, "I need to examine her to help her, Alpha."

It was not enough. For how much I knew he needed to look at her...touch her. My wolf would not allow it. We struggled internally for a battle of control, one that I could feel myself losing. My canines began to lengthen as my wolf took over. At the sound of the front door opening, my head whipped around, ready to take on the enemy. Oakley appeared at the doorway. I growled deeply at him, and his eyes widened. He dropped his head and raised his hands in a defensive gesture. Another growl ripped from my throat. I could feel my eyes turning black with my slip in control. I pleaded with it in my mind to let them help her, but he could not be swayed.

Oakley glanced at the doctor, who said hushedly, "He will not let me approach her. I need to examine the girl."

The first pop in my spine signaled my impending shift.

"Alpha, you do not want to hurt the Luna by shifting so close to her. It would be best if you went outside to do so safely. I will guard her with my life."

Another sound at the door broke my concentration at his words.

"I will guard her, Alpha. It is my duty and an honor," August said, walking in without an ounce of hesitation.

Finally, some reason found its way to my wolf. I turned and darted out of the room, shifting in the lobby before pushing out the doors. Standing guard, my wolf paced back and forth in front of the building. Even he knew that they were right. I could not shift in there. I could have hurt her with one of my claws as they sprouted from my hands as I changed. I needed to satisfy him so that he would allow me to regain control. I wanted to be in there with her, to hold her hand and comfort her. Mates helped the healing process. I could help her, but not like this. He finally seemed to understand the situation and released his grasp on me, allowing me to shift back to my human form. I wasted no time going back in.

Dr. Stone shone a small pen light into her eye, which he held open. The new mate mark on her shoulder was proudly displayed through her tattered shirt, confirming that she was their Luna. Not that my scent, which was now mixed with hers, would have caused any doubt. Dr. Stone looked at me worriedly as I walked over to her, holding her tiny hand with my own. He stepped back, lowering his head to me.

"She has suffered a traumatic brain injury. From Beta Oakley's description, she has been unconscious for over an hour at this point. I will need to observe her until she wakes. I must tell you, Alpha, humans are more susceptible to negative effects from this type of injury. We do not know how long she will be out."

My wolf stirred in me once more. I held my tongue, nodding at him, and pulled a chair to her side, holding her hand for dear life. Hopefully, my proximity would help her heal. Dr. Stone quietly left the room, leaving the four of us inside.

"What happened? Why did she leave?" Oakley asked from his place by the door.

"You were right. I should never have allowed Sienna in," I confessed.

I could see their shoulders tense.

"Did she do something to her?" August asked with a hint of danger in his tone.

"Not directly. She's been moving her clothes into the Luna's closet. Juniper found them and assumed I was in a relationship with her."

I didn't want to look at their expressions. I didn't want to see the 'told you so' on their faces. Admitting that I had been wrong was hard enough. I would not be able to stand their accusing stares. Dr. Stone walked in with a bowl of warm water and a few towels.

"I thought that you would like to clean her up," he said as he pulled a fresh gown off his arm, laying it on the foot of the bed.

August and Oakley left the room after Dr. Stone, closing the door behind themselves. I found a pair of scissors on a tray next to the bed and used them to cut away what remained of her clothing. The forest had not been kind to her, as evidenced by its destruction. My eyes roamed down her body, noting each new scrape and bruise. Her head had a fresh bandage wrapped around it. I dipped a towel in the warm water and carefully wiped her skin. It was covered in mud with a few small leaves that had stuck to it. Once I was satisfied with the cleaning, I used some antiseptic spray on her cuts to help prevent any infection. I stripped the bed from underneath her, being careful to lift her in the process as gently as possible so as not to stir her. It was damp and dirty from when I brought her in. I replaced it with a clean sheet and finally wrapped the gown around her, pulling the blanket over her. Her body still felt cold to the touch. I lay down next to her on the side of the bed, willing my warmth into her. It was here that I decided I would stay until she woke.

15

Juniper

I felt warmth radiating from my side. It was so comfortable I thought I could stay there forever. My eyes fluttered open, revealing a dark room. A light showed in from under a door to my right, giving just enough illumination to take in my surroundings. I didn't recognize it. How did I get here? I looked at the warm mass lying next to me. Forest was asleep with his arm wrapped across my waist. His head rested on his bicep while the rest of his arm awkwardly wrapped over my head. He must have been the warmth I had felt. I smiled over at him, watching his sleeping face. I tried to sit up, but my body protested. A sharp pain stung in my head. I put my hand up, wincing from the contact, to find it wrapped in a bandage. What happened? Why is my head wrapped, and why does it hurt so bad? My movement must have woken Forest as his eyes shot open, and he quickly sat up.

"You're awake," he leaned down, kissing my lips.

The now familiar tingling feeling rolled through me. He sat

back up and looked carefully over me as if I were a delicate flower not to be crushed.

"How are you feeling?" His concern for me was thick as he asked.

"My head hurts. What happened?" I asked while I tried to sit up again, but slowed as my head spun.

"Careful. Let me help you."

He lifted me gently and readjusted the pillows behind me so I could lean back on them. Once I was settled, he sat in a chair next to the bed and took my hand.

"You fell and hit your head on a rock."

"I don't remember it happening," I confessed as I reached up with my free hand and inspected the bandage around it.

He rubbed his thumb on my hand in a comforting gesture.

"Let me get the doctor to look you over."

He kissed the back of my hand before walking to the door. I squinted from the light pouring in from outside. I heard his voice from a different room, farther away. I noticed a tall brunette standing outside the door. He faced away from me so I could not see his features. He seemed familiar, but I wasn't sure where I had seen him before. Two sets of footsteps came down the hall. Forest and an older man with greying hair and welcoming eyes walked in, flipping a light on.

"I'm glad to see you awake, Luna. I'm Dr. Stone," the older man introduced himself.

"Oh, my name is Jumper." I corrected him.

He smiled kindly at me. I had never seen a doctor before. The healers at the coven had always treated my ailments.

"May I?" he asked, gesturing to my head.

"Sure."

He looked back at Forest, who gave a slight nod and walked to the bedside, pulling back the bandage. He readjusted it into place and pulled what looked like a pen out of his pocket, turning it on like a flashlight. He shone it in one eye after the other before stepping back.

"You suffered a moderate brain injury after you fell and hit your head. You have been unconscious for just over four hours. I want to keep you here for observation for the next day to watch for any other symptoms to arise."

"Okay..." I said, uncertain.

Forest rubbed my shoulder in reassurance, and I relaxed.

"Now, I know you just woke up, but are you feeling any dizziness or confusion?"

"I mean, all of this is new, but I don't feel confused by where I am."

I knew I was at some type of doctor's office or hospital. I'd seen a few movies over the years with the same stark white walls and colorful laminate floors next to the medical bed, and a few tools nearby were a dead giveaway.

"And dizziness?"

"I was a little dizzy when I sat up, but I'm feeling fine now."

"Good. It would be best to move slowly to be sure not to bring on another spell. Can you tell me how you were injured?"

"I honestly don't remember."

"What is the last thing you remember?"

I bit my lip as I tried to recall. Did he know about wolves? I wasn't sure how much to tell him.

"It's okay, Juniper. He's one of us," Forest said softly as if he could read my mind.

I looked over to him for clarification.

"He's a wolf."

"Oh, okay, um...I rode on Forest's back to the edge of the village. He grabbed some pants from a box next to a tree. I know we started walking into the village, but that's all I remember."

Dr. Stone glanced over at Forest, who stared back at him. His shoulders were tensed. They looked like they were having an unspoken conversation with each other. Was he mind-linking him as he did me?

"If you two are talking, I'd like to be included," my frustration getting the best of me. "It does concern me, doesn't it?" I added glaring daggers at them both.

"It appears that you have lost several hours of your memory. I don't want you to worry. Some amnesia is common after a brain injury. Your memories should return within a day or two."

"That's good, I guess."

"I will let you rest now. Would you like me to send for any food for you two?"

"I'm fine, thank you," I responded.

After he left, I looked over to Forest, who was staring at the door. He seemed anxious, which was fitting because I felt an unfamiliar anxiety in my chest. After a moment, he looked down at me and smiled.

"So what did I miss?" I joked at him.

His smile fell, and a worried look crossed his face.

"Do you remember me telling you about being an Alpha?"

"No. What's an Alpha?"

He explained to me the hierarchy of werewolf packs. I was stunned to learn that he was the leader, though I guess he had already told me before this stint of amnesia took hold of me. I wished that I could remember. He still had not gotten to the way I hit my head, which was aggravating me. He kept telling me small things we supposedly had talked about.

I stopped him in the middle of describing his apartment, well, our apartment, which he made sure to point out. "Forest, I appreciate you filling me in on all the small details, but you still haven't told me how I hit my head."

He ran his hand back through his hair. "The doctor said not to stress you out."

"And you think it will?" It seemed like something serious had happened, which only piqued my interest further. "I want to know."

"I think we should ask the doctor first."

"Forest," I said sternly.

I was now determined to find out exactly what had happened. He let a deep sigh out.

"You left. You ran out into the forest. I assume you were trying to go back to the Harper cabin. You agreed to come back and talk to me, but you must have tripped and hit your head on a rock. "

"That makes no sense. Why would I leave? Even the thought makes my chest tighten," I said, rubbing my fist to my breast.

I could tell he was hesitant. Whatever had happened would have been bad for me to leave. I held onto his hand a little tighter.

"Please, tell me why I left."

"Before I saw you, there were others."

"Other what?" I asked, clueless as to what he was referring to.

"I had other women in my life. One in particular that I spent more time with."

My breath caught in my throat. A swirl of anger and sadness twisted in my gut.

"They were never serious," He quickly added, watching my response. "I'm being truthful when I tell you that they meant absolutely nothing to me, nor I to them. It was simply responding to the primal calls of our bodies."

"How many?" I asked with anger.

"Do you think that's important?"

"Yes!" I shouted, "It is important. You were my first, and I went against my family to be with you. It's not like we have mates or husbands back at the coven. There is not a line of men waiting at my doorstep back home for me to jump if I want to get laid. Most of the women from my coven have only been with one or two men. It matters to me, Forest."

I wasn't even sure where this jealous rage was coming from. I had never expected to be in a relationship, and I knew enough to know that it was not unusual for humans to date around, but the thought of him with other women ignited a fire within me.

"I'm sorry, Juniper. It is one of my biggest regrets not waiting for you," he said mournfully.

He peppered my hand in kisses as he pleaded for my forgiveness. I felt betrayed, even though I knew there was no standing for it. I knew people outside the coven had multiple relationships; it's just...he was mine. All mine. I had never experienced jealousy before this day, but this was one hell of an introduction to it. My guts felt like they had been ripped out and twisted in a knot. Even breathing felt like a chore. Tears pricked at my eyes.

"Please, just give me some time by myself," I said, turning away from him.

"Don't send me away, not like this. Not while you're hurt and in the clinic," he pleaded, but I kept my back to him. "At least let me stay in the lobby."

I needed space, but I still did not want him far away.

"Fine. But do not come back in until I am ready," I spoke to the wall.

"I promise," he whispered before leaving.

16

Forest

I walked out of Juniper's room to find August standing guard outside. The same place he had stood since she was brought in. It made me feel better that he had never faltered from his responsibilities. I didn't expect him to move until she ordered him to or when she was discharged.

"Do not let anyone inside, not even the doctor, without my approval. And make sure she doesn't leave," I commanded.

"Yes, Alpha," he bowed his head as he confirmed my orders.

I was scared that she would run again. She was clearly upset, as I would be if our roles were reversed. Being mated to someone was completely different than any human relationship. Knowing that your mate has been with another can be accepted, but the thought would be painful. Many wolves waited for their mate, knowing how territorial we were over them. I grew angry at myself for being so thoughtless to my future mate and to the women I had slept with. They had mates out there as well, and our promiscuous activities would hurt them, too. For now, I needed to give Juniper time to accept it, but it chewed away at me not being by her side. When I came to the lobby, I could see the first glimpse of color in the sky as the sun worked its way to the horizon. I was exhausted, both mentally and physically. I knew that the pack would be buzzing with gossip after last night. Word that I had found my Luna would spread like wildfire after I had to call so many warriors to save her from her family and search for her in the forest.

Dr. Stone sat at the desk behind the counter where people would check in, working on the computer. Oakley sat against the far wall, asleep in his chair. I sat next to him, waking him from his slumber. He jolted up and looked around wide-eyed. He rubbed his eyes with his fingers before looking at me.

"How's she doing?" he asked grogily.

"She's awake."

"That's good news!" he said, perking up.

"It is," I said, slightly hopeful.

"Do you want to talk about it?"

"No," I replied sternly.

Short and to the point. I did not want to talk about it. I didn't want to be living it, but here I was. It was a nightmare. I was sitting on the edge of a cliff, waiting for my world to come crashing down around me. Everything I dreamt of for my whole life was squashed under the thumb of karma. I scratched the back of my head and rested my chin on my fist. Oakley patted my back a few times and sat back, crossing his arms in front of him. I looked in his direction.

"Did you talk to Sienna last night?"

His eyes widened.

"I did not," he said, emphasizing each word as if he was just remembering, "but I will go first thing this morning."

"It is the first thing…"

"Right. I'll be back." He stood from the chair, stretching quickly before leaving.

I leaned back, my mind full of what-ifs. How had I managed to screw up my mating with Juniper in less than a day?

An hour later, Oakley returned, reclaiming his seat at my side. I could see the first few people making their way out and about for the day. Seeing me sitting in the clinic was sure to fuel the chatter that I was sure had already started. Dr. Stone had gone to lie down in one of the free rooms and rest. If I listened closely, I could hear Juniper's breath. She had not fallen back asleep. I could feel the onslaught of emotions coming from. I wasn't sure if she could feel mine. She had never mentioned anything. Wolves could feel their mate through their bond, both their emotions and their pain. It was how I knew she was in trouble last night. I caught Oakley watching me.

"What?" I asked with annoyance.

"I wasn't sure if you would want to know how it went."

"Not really, but I guess lay it on me."

"It did not go well..." he slowly let out. "It was worse than I expected."

That caught my attention, "What happened?"

"Well, first, may I say that she is not a nice person to wake up. I don't know how you woke up to her all those mornings. She has a particular funk."

I cut him off, "Get on with it."

"Sorry. Anyway, I let her know that you had found your mate and that she needed to stay clear of you both. She was on the verge of shifting from her anger. She screamed at me that you couldn't do that, and you were hers, and she would make that little bitch pay."

"Watch your mouth," I growled at him in warning.

He raised his hands, "Her words, not mine. I'm just letting you know. I wouldn't put it past her to do something."

This was the last thing I needed to deal with right now.

"Get a tail on her. I want to know everywhere she goes and everything she does until I can get things sorted."

"Sure thing," he said, saluting me with his hand.

I leaned back in my chair, but saw him continue staring at me.

"Is there something else?"

"Yeah," He drew out. "On my walk to and from Sienna's house, I caught whispers from the pack. There's word that you found your mate. Supposedly, she was being hunted down by witches. I think you need to address the pack. You know how quickly gossip can turn."

"Fuck...," I leaned my head down and ran my hand up my hair. "Fine... Call a meeting for this evening. I don't want to leave Juniper yet."

"Right-e-o, Alpha. I'm on it."

"And one more thing, will you search my apartment for anything Sienna may have left there and toss it?"

He smiled with malevolent intent across his face, "With pleasure."

He stood and looked back at me, giving me two thumbs up before leaving again. He was a great Beta and one of my best friends, but his lackadaisical approach sometimes got under my skin. He could never quite decipher when the time was or wasn't appropriate for his banter.

17

Juniper

I couldn't quite tell how I was feeling. My rational side argued that I was harsh on Forest for having other partners. He said that they were purely physical. From my limited knowledge of men, it was normal for them to sleep around. And the coven was not known for being committed in a relationship, as in, never...But it still hurt. I felt like there was something he left out. Possibly why I felt so passionately about it. I needed to accept that he had other partners before we continued our conversation. I didn't want to act rashly from how fueled I was already.

I rolled onto my side and pulled my blanket high over my shoulder as if it were some childhood security object. I looked out the window to my side and watched the world visible through the slats grow in color from the rising sunlight. I wanted Forest to come in with me, be near me, but I wasn't ready yet. I hated feeling this way. I heard a knock at the door and rolled over.

"Come in," I croaked, clearing hoarseness from my throat.

A tall, middle-aged woman with black hair twisted up and

pinned in a bun on her head came in. She was wearing light blue scrubs and a stethoscope draped over her neck. Was everyone in this pack so tall? I felt dwarfed by every person I had seen here. And don't get me started on their looks. Every man and woman were the epitome of beauty. Even the woman who stood before me, whom I guessed was in her mid-forties, dripped with sex appeal.

"Good morning, Luna," she said.

I went to correct her, telling her my name when I recalled my conversation with Forest. Luna was the term for the lead female of the pack, which I guess was me now. How would a pack of were-wolves even take a witch as one of their leaders? I refocused on the woman who was waiting for my reply.

"Good morning," I said quickly, trying to cover up my distracted thoughts.

"My name is Aurora. I'll be your nurse today," she introduced herself.

She walked over and took hold of my wrist, eyeing her watch.

"How are you feeling at the moment?"

"Sore," I admitted.

"I bet, after a hit like that. Let me take a look at your laceration."

She pulled the bandage down and inspected my injury.

"It seems to be healing quickly. I didn't expect it to have healed as much as it has. When did you hurt yourself again?" She asked, picking a chart off the wall near my head.

"Last night."

"Hmm. I think I'll ask the doctor to look at it."

"Is there something wrong?"

"Not at all! It's healing much faster than I expected from a human."

What was that supposed to mean? Do they heal differently from humans? Witches are nearly identical to humans physically.

She smiled at me before she left, leaving me to think what it could mean. I felt a wave of anxiety roll through me that was not my own. Why did this keep happening? I should ask the doctor about it. As if on cue, Dr. Stone came in.

"Aurora told me that you are healing quicker than normal. I would like to take a look," he asked.

"Sure."

Once again, the bandage was peeled back.

"Hmm, yes. It appears she is right. I don't think you need this anymore." He unwrapped the bandage from my head and discarded it in a red bin on the side of the room.

"How are you feeling?"

"Sore," I repeated.

"Just your head?"

"My whole body is," I explained.

He listened to my heart and lungs before looking into my eyes with his light again.

"Do you normally heal quickly?"

"No. At least, not that I know of. Do wolves heal differently?"

"Yes. Wolves have a type of rapid healing. Similar to what you have experienced with that gash on your head. It's nearly gone."

I ran my fingers over the skin, feeling no scabs or cuts.

I sat upright, "What does this mean?"

"I honestly don't know. Two other humans are mated to wolves in the pack that I see in the clinic. Neither of them has developed any changes such as this. This may be personal, but may I ask you how you and the Alpha found each other?"

My cheeks blushed as the memory came to me. "I felt a pull to the forest. He was in a meadow as his wolf."

"Did he scare you?"

"No, actually quite the opposite. I was mesmerized by him."

"Very interesting," he said as he looked at me with a new look.

"What is?"

I wished he would say what he was getting at.

"It seems you are true mates, paired by the Moon Goddess herself. I've never heard of a human and a shifter being true mates before."

"Ever?" I asked.

"No. Perhaps because you are mated to an Alpha, he was able to pass on some of his gifts to you. I will need to do some research and look further into it."

"Okay. Will you please let me know what you find?"

"Of course."

He started to walk towards the door, and I remembered I was going to ask him about my strange emotions.

"Dr. Stone..."

He turned around and looked at me.

"I have one other thing I wanted to ask you about."

He smiled and returned to my side, "Sure, you can ask me anything."

"I appreciate that. My mind seems to be full of questions."

"That is to be expected, being thrust into a completely new world."

I smiled at him. "I...I've had these feelings."

His eyebrows scrunched together a little, "What type of feelings?"

"Emotions. But they don't feel like my own. It's like I am feeling someone else."

He was going to think I was crazy. Maybe I was.

"Very interesting..." He said, crossing his arms over his chest. "Another common trait between mated pairs is to feel what the other does. You are deeply connected. We don't say it's two halves of the same soul for nothing."

"So, what I'm feeling are Forest's emotions?"

"I guess there is only one way to tell."

"What's that?"

"We can run a little experiment..."

He seemed more excited than he should be at his request. I cocked my eyebrow at him.

"Nothing bad, I promise," he chuckled. "I know that you asked him to wait in the lobby. He would most certainly be in here in any other circumstance. If you're willing, I will go out there and tell him you would like to speak to him. See if you can sense his feelings from it. Focus on him. It should help you decipher if it is coming from him or something else."

Was I ready to talk to him? I knew the answer, but I needed to accept it.

"Okay. Let's do it," I said hesitantly.

He smiled at me and left, closing the door behind him. A minute later, I felt a mix of joy and nervousness. I focused on Forest the same way I did when I would talk to him through my mind. It struck me that it was him that I felt. I felt sad that he had been in as much emotional turmoil as I had. His nervousness increased. Was he feeling mine right now? A soft knock echoed from the door, and I straightened myself up.

"Come in," I called.

Forest walked in, watching me. His nerves were skyrocketing, but I also felt something else...something more substantial. It was not a feeling. It was warm and comforting. It filled me with joy. I realized that it was his love for me. He loved me. How had I not noticed that before? I remember traces of it, but now that I was focusing on it, it was all-consuming. Love...It was something I never thought I would feel for another. I mean, yes, I loved my family, but this was different. It was stronger. Like, I wanted to spend every moment with him for the rest of my life and tell him all my secrets. How could I feel this strongly for someone so fast? I had only met him the day before, but there was no doubt that I loved him.

A smile spread across his face, and his pace quickened, sitting on the side of my bed and taking my hands in his.

"In all my years, I have never seen something like this." Dr. Stone said from the doorway.

He walked in and closed the door behind him. Forest looked at him suspiciously.

"It appears your mate has picked up on some of your wolf abilities."

Forest looked back at me and noticed the healing skin on my head.

Shocked, he said, "She's healed."

"Yes, and it appears that she can feel you."

"And link me," He added, looking at me with amazement. "That's simply amazing."

"Do you know why she can do all of these things?"

"Not one clue," Dr. Stone laughed. "But I already informed the Luna that I will look more into it."

"That would be great," He paused and looked at me, asking me silently if he could share my secret with him.

I nodded, telling him he could.

"I think I need to tell you...Juniper is not human."

"She's not?" He seemed surprised. "Everything about her, besides these new abilities, appears human to me. Even her blood work came back as a human."

"She's actually a witch."

Dr. Stone's mouth dropped open. "I've never met a witch before, and most definitely have never heard of a wolf being mated to one. That's quite interesting."

He paced the room, stoking his goatee.

"Is that a problem?" Forest came off almost threatening.

"Oh, not a problem at all," Dr. Stone tried to diffuse the situation. "I was just thinking if that would explain the changes. I have only read of witches. I know they were created by the Moon Goddess, just as we were. Is that correct?"

"Yes. The story we were taught was that thousands of years ago, when humans still worshipped the old gods, they had erected a temple to the Moon Goddess atop a hill. She goes by many names, but most know her as Selene today. A foreign religion had started to take root in the town nearby, and their zealots decided to burn her temple down with all of her followers inside as an act of defiance against their beliefs. She was so angered that she took the four women who miraculously survived and bestowed a piece of her power within them. She instructed them to protect those who wished to follow her. She told them that, for their service, she would pass their gift down to their children. Since all of the attackers were male, she deemed that no man would retain the gifts and, in due course, made it so each woman would only birth females, allowing her magic to be passed from one generation to the next."

They both looked at me with wonder in their eyes.

"I had never heard the origin story," Forest commented.

"So, if I am understanding this right, witches hold the power of Selene?"

"Just part of it. We pull energy from her by pledging our devotion every full moon. With it, though, we can also pull energy from the nature she's touched, which is why we worship both the moon and the earth."

"How do you pull power from the earth?" Dr. Stone questioned further.

"Little ways, but water is the most powerful besides the moon. It is strongly connected to the moon, bringing in the tide and rereleasing it."

"I can learn a lot from you, Luna."

I smiled at the doctor whose bright and excited face filled my heart with acceptance and the happiness that comes from it. I locked eyes with Forest, who looked as bewildered as the older man beside him.

"Well...You are clear to leave since you seem to have healed up. I would still like you to take it easy for a few days. I would like you to return if you suffer any dizziness, confusion, or headaches."

"Of course. Thank you for taking care of me."

"It has been my pleasure. And may I say...welcome to the West Moon Pack."

My smile could not have been larger. "Thank you."

18

Juniper

I took a quick shower in the ensuite bathroom in my room at the clinic before we left. I could still feel the grittiness of the dirt that covered me from last night. When I asked if my clothes survived, Forest shared that he had cut what little remained when he washed me. After his confession of cleaning my nude body, while I lay asleep, my cheeks reddened. He had already seen all of me in the meadow, and nudity was not uncommon for me, but what he did was highly intimate, especially from a man. Before I stepped into the shower, he told me that he would find some clothes for me. I was surprised when I came out to find a short-sleeved white sundress with dark wooden buttons up to its entire length. I wondered where he found it so quickly, but remembered that they had shops in their town. He must have run over to one of them while I washed. Next to it was a simple white cotton bra and pantie set. He must have remembered what I wore yesterday because these were pretty similar.

As I dropped the towel and slid the bra on, a picture of a black lace bra flashed through my head. I remembered holding it, but had never owned something of that fashion. I couldn't imagine what my Gran would have said if she had found something like that in the laundry. The thought of my Gran brought me sadness. Would I ever see her again? A soft knock came from the door before Forest walked in. He eyed me carefully.

"What's wrong?" he asked softly.

"It's nothing," I said dismissively.

"No. Don't pull that with me. I can feel it, remember."

"I just miss my family," I could feel his panic rise again. "Calm down. I'm not going anywhere. I miss them. I don't know if I will ever see them again."

"You will," he said with conviction. "We will find a way for you to connect with them. Maybe you can give them a call?"

"I don't know their numbers. I've never had to call them before. Phones, in general, are not common among my people; there are just a few landlines to get by."

"Is there someplace they go? Maybe we can look up a number."

"Heather has an online store. Maybe I can message her through that, though...I'm not sure where we stand after last night."

He pulled me against his chest, wrapping his arms around me. "We'll think about it and come up with a plan."

"Thank you," I whispered.

He kissed my head before stepping back, "Now I think you should get dressed. Seeing you like this is making me hard."

I looked at him funny before noticing the growing bulge in his pants. Recalling our moments of passion from yesterday lit a fire within me. I wanted that again. I heard a low grumble come from him and looked into his eyes. They had darkened from their usual grey to almost black. I realized that he wanted me as much as I wanted him. I bit my lip in anticipation of what he might do. Part of me wanted him to take me right here, while the other thought about how terrible an idea that was. He adjusted himself and stepped back.

"I will wait outside the door. I don't think I can control myself if I stay."

I hid my smile behind my hand as he hastily left the room. I turned back and finished dressing. When I opened the door, I found the large frame of my mate blocking the door.

"What are you doing?"

"Making sure no one went in."

"Would they do that? They've already released me."

"I'm not taking any chances," he declared.

I giggled at his overprotectiveness but slipped my hand into his as we walked into the clinic lobby. It had the same white walls and colorful floors as the room I had been staying in—a handful of basic wooden chairs with teal cushioning placed around the room in rows. The whole left wall had giant windows looking out on a street with a small crowd gathered outside. I wondered what they were doing. A window was cut into a wall to my right. Aurora stood behind it, watching us.

"Goodbye Alpha...Luna."

"Thank you, Aurora," Forest replied.

He turned towards me, "Juniper, the pack has heard I found you. They are all interested, and they have been gathering outside."

I let out a shaky breath and felt my pulse quicken. The crowd I could see over Forest's shoulder was there for me.

"When we go out. I will make an announcement introducing you as my Luna. You do not have to say anything. I want you to be prepared for it."

Be prepared for an announcement to a large crowd of strangers, shifter strangers at that, informing them that I am to help lead them... This was way beyond my comfort zone, but realizing there was no way around it, I had to suck it up. I bit my lip and held his hand a little tighter. At my gesture, he turned and led us out the doors. We stopped on the sidewalk out front. The low murmur of conversation quieted.

Forest stood tall and projected his deep voice in a way so everyone could hear, "As you all may have heard, I have found my mate. This is Juniper, your Luna. She has had a difficult few days, and I ask that you give her time to recover and adjust to the pack before approaching her. I will be having a meeting tonight at seven to announce her officially."

With that, he pulled me forward, the crowd parting for us. I could hear the slight hum of conversations return. I heard a scuffle nearby and craned my neck to see what it was, but I couldn't see past the crowd, and Forest never slowed in his step, so I turned back around, making sure not to trip.

For the entirety of the walk through the town, I felt eyes on me and could hear the whispers. It sent an unease through me, making me nervous. I had hoped that everyone would be like Dr. Stone and welcome me with open arms, but I was unsure after this. We approached a mansion with a circular drive. I slightly remembered it from last night. We walked straight in the front doors, finding two men standing at the base of one of the staircases.

"Juniper, I want you to meet my Beta, Oakley, and my Gamma, August."

They both bowed their heads to me.

"Hi," I said awkwardly.

They both seemed familiar, but it was like a memory just out of my grasp.

"Welcome, Luna," August said in a heartfelt tone.

"We sure are glad you're here. This one has been going mad with you in the clinic," the other said, teasing Forest.

"Thanks. I'm glad to be out of there, too."

"We will be up in our apartment for the day. Juniper needs to rest, so I do not want anyone disturbing us. I will meet you at the meeting tonight."

"You two kids have fun now," he teased us.

If eyes could throw daggers, Oakley would be riddled with them from the look Forest shot him. We walked up several sets of stairs and entered the double doors at the top.

"Do you remember the apartment?" Forest asked softly once we were inside.

"I think so, but not really. Everything feels like it's on the tip of my tongue...or brain, I guess. I just can't put it together."

"Don't try too hard. It will all come back in due time."

I welcomed his attempt to assure me, but it still bothered me. He led me into an ample open-concept living space, sitting on the sofa to one side. He looked at me nervously.

"Why are you anxious?" I asked, both worried and concerned.

He sighed and ran his hand down his face. "I don't want you to leave."

"Okay," I asked nervously, "Is there something I need to know?"

"I just want to be open with you."

"I would like that to..."

I felt like he was building up to telling me something horrible; my nerves flared the longer he took.

"I told you how there were others before you, but I told you none of them were serious.

"Yes..."

"There was one; her name was Sienna," he sighed again. "She may have been more attached to me, but it was more for the social standing that came from being with an Alpha. People favor you and know not to cross you."

"Okay, why are you telling me more about her now?"

"I had been seeing her up until I met you. I hadn't realized how much of a claim she had been taking on your position. She had slowly been moving her stuff into my apartment. I knew she had one or two necessities, but we found more, lots more. It seems that she had moved in a substantial amount of her stuff here. Clothes, personal items.... She kept them hidden from me so that I wouldn't notice."

He looked at me. I had already come to terms with the fact that he had other women before me, realizing that it was a bit overdramatic to think that a twenty-six-year-old man would have waited for a mate he never knew was coming, but it still hurt a little. I couldn't even explain why.

He continued, "I just wanted to be upfront with you. I asked Oakley to clear out her stuff, but based on how much she had hidden, I didn't want you to find something and think there was more to it. If I have to lay every secret I have ever had on the table for you, I will."

I ran my hand down his cheek, and he looked into my eyes, "Thank you for telling me. I feel like being honest with each other will make it work between us. I can already feel your emotions, but while it is a gift, it can fill me with doubts and concerns. When I feel you are nervous or sad, it makes me wonder if I have done something. We will get to know each other better and how we work, but let's be as open as possible for now. If you are ever wondering what is happening with me, ask, and I will do the same for you."

Relief poured over his face, and he smirked at me, "You really are perfect."

He leaned forward and kissed my lips gently. Butterflies filled my stomach, and I tightened my arms around his neck. Our light and gentle kisses quickly deepened, becoming more fevered and passionate. Our hands began roaming each other's bodies. A fire started to grow inside of me. He pulled back, catching me off guard.

"Why did you stop?" I asked, out of breath

"We shouldn't, not right now. You should be resting."

"I feel fine," I laughed out.

"Please?" he asked. "I was so scared last night. If there is even a chance that you could be hurt, I think we should wait. Just a day or two."

I sighed, frustrated, "Alright, I guess so."

He cocked a smile at my pouted lips.

"Don't think for a second that once you are better, I won't lock you in this apartment and ravage you for days," he said, kissing my neck.

A shiver ran up my spine, and I leaned my head back, giving him better access.

"You can't expect me to stop when you're teasing me like this."

He grumbled but pulled away, "You're right, I'm sorry."

Instead of throwing ourselves to our desires, we sat for the next several hours, getting to know each other. He told me all about how his mother died when he was young. She sacrificed herself to save a group of pups from a rogue attack. He then had to explain to me what a rogue was. They were shifters who lost their pack for one reason or another. They tend to be more feral. Wolves, in particular, need the connection of a pack and an Alpha's command to be grounded. They become impulsive and have difficulty managing in the human world without it, often finding their way back into the wild. They can become enraged and jealous of what a pack offers, and that impulsiveness can cause them to act rashly, usually attacking pack wolves when they see them out of spite or rage.

He went on to explain to me about his father's death and how he had stepped into the Alpha role. He was only twenty-four when it happened. He told me how most Alphas stepped down when their heirs were in their late twenties or early thirties. It was when a wolf had passed the immaturity of youth but still wielded his strength to its maximum capabilities.

After his life story and some explanations of pack life, I told him about my story. I could feel his anger when I told him what had happened to my mother. I explained to him what our daily life looked like at the settlement and how we worshipped the full moon, dancing naked beneath Selene's moon to absorb as much from her as we could, which caused him to glance at me with a sinful gaze.

"That won't happen here, at least not with the pack around," he said with a chuckle.

I giggled at him, "Nearly every time I have seen you, you were butt naked. Obviously, nudity is not looked down upon here."

"That's different," he said defensively.

"Why? Because you're a man."

"No. Because you're mine, nobody else can see your body."

"And what about yours?" I asked with a coked eyebrow, "Isn't your body mine?"

"Yes, but it's not like I walk through the village like that. We have boxes of clothing to change into. You've just seen me where there are none."

"How about this: I won't dance around nude in front of everyone on the full moons, and you keep a pair of pants close by."

"Deal," he said, kissing me.

There was a soft knock on the door. Forest stood and answered it. I could hear whispers coming from the doorway before he returned.

"I need to go. There is a meeting tonight to tell the pack about you."

"Am I going?" I asked, feeling nervous about facing his pack for the first time.

"You can stay here and rest. It's more informational than an official meeting. We should introduce you to them in the next week or so."

"I can go now."

Anxiety nipped in my stomach, but if I was going to make the West Moon Pack my home, I should not hide from meeting its people.

He glanced me over, "Are you sure?"

"Yes," I said, trying to convey confidence in my voice.

"Let's go then."

He helped me up. August was waiting outside the door for us. He looked surprised to see me.

"Luna," he said, lowering his head to me briefly. "Will you be joining us?"

"Yeah, figured I'd meet the in-laws."

I caught a glimpse of a smile before he turned around and led us out of the pack house.

19

Forest

ugust had to come to get me for the meeting because I
had been lost in my conversation with Juniper and was
now running late. I assumed that Oakley was there,
filling the time with whatever bullshit pack business he could
come up with. I was surprised when Juniper said she would join
me. It was just another thing she did that showed me how great
she would be as Luna. She didn't shy away from uncomfortable
situations but instead faced them head-on. I had to admit, I would
have preferred to keep us locked up in the apartment for the next
week, getting to know each other in all sorts of ways, but after last
night, word had spread around about her and the involvement of
witches, and I needed to put the pack's fears and questions to rest.

I still wasn't sure what I would say about her origins. Was she
even alright having others know about her being a witch? I figured
it would both help her and hurt her in the initial acceptance.
While I expected most of the pack to accept her regardless, I knew
there would be a few who were upset that she was not a wolf. It

would soften the blow if I could reason with them that she holds some of the Moon Goddess's power.

"Hey, I need to ask what you are comfortable sharing with the pack?"

"You mean, can they know I'm a witch?"

"Yeah, if it's alright, or should we keep it to ourselves?"

"If I'm going to live here, they will figure it out. While we do not discuss it with humans, I assume I can share it with your pack. You all are in a similar situation after all."

"Fair enough. When we get there, I will address the pack. There is no need to talk unless you want to."

We entered through the back door of the community hall. It was where we hosted pack-wide events such as meetings and celebrations. It was a substantially sized square building with a decorative facade, grand arch, and large windows. We walked down the dimly lit back hallway and to the side of the theater-style stage. It was a bit reminiscent of a community theater or human high school, but we found it fit the needs required from it well. We stood to the side of the stage, hidden behind a heavy black velvet curtain. I could make out the rows of folding chairs that had been set up and were filled with the familiar faces of our community. When Oakley spotted me, he ended his speech and introduced me.

"I will talk to them first before calling you out."

"O-okay," she stuttered. I could tell this situation spiked some nerves for her. It would have been easier for her to walk out with me as support, but I wanted to get a read on the crowd before I fully exposed her. I walked to the center of the stage. We didn't need microphones since all wolves had enhanced hearing. It only became difficult for those in the back to hear when the crowd became rowdy, which I hoped tonight wouldn't be one of those instances.

"West Moon, thank you for gathering tonight. I have called this meeting to announce that I have found my mate!"

I could see excited smiles around the room, but they waited to celebrate until I had finished.

"She is wonderful, and I am positive that she will fill the role of Luna beyond our expectations. As some may have heard, there was some activity that required our warriors to join us. I have heard the gossip that has spread throughout the village, and I want to stop the speculations."

I looked over at Juniper, who was fiddling with her hands and watching me and the crowd.

"My mate, Juniper, is not a shifter," I announced.

Gasps and other sounds of disbelief spread through the crowd. My pulse quickened at the anticipation of revealing what Juniper was. I raised my hand to quiet the whispers.

"I know it may come as a surprise that she is not, and I understand that, but let me finish. She is not a shifter, but she is not human. I was also surprised to learn that she is, in fact, a witch."

The crowd stirred. The sea of whispers and talking returned. A few began to get louder at their shock.

"How do we know she is safe?" A woman called out from the side.

"How do you know she hasn't cast a love spell on you?" A man accused.

"What if she casts a spell on you to wipe out the pack?"

"That is enough!" I commanded, my voice dripping with authority.

"She has not cast a spell on me. I am positive. I will not allow these accusations against your Luna to continue. You will respect her."

Everyone's heads dropped as their alpha criticized their behavior.

"If I may?" Dr. Stone stood in the crowd, raising his hand.

"Dr. Stone, you have the floor." I offered it up, knowing what he had seen, hoping that he could calm some of the pack's fears.

"I treated the Luna overnight. I have detected no ill intention and believe the Moon Goddess paired our Alpha and her together. Only a true connection like the one I witnessed would have helped the Luna heal from her accident last night. I understand that witches, at least moon witches such as the Luna, worship the Moon Goddess as we do. Beyond that, the power that she yields was gifted to them directly from the Moon Goddess as a means to protect her followers. I believe that she was sent to us to protect us in a way that we cannot do ourselves. I will also attest to her character. She is a kind, forgiving, and patient person. Just what we need in a Luna."

I couldn't have said it better myself. I could see the relief flood the eyes of my pack members. I looked over and saw the same relief on Juniper's face.

"Thank you, Dr. Stone."

I walked to the side and grabbed Juniper's hand, leading her back out.

"Now, may I officially introduce you all to Juniper, your Luna."

I could nearly feel the breath she was holding as she walked out on stage in front of all eight hundred and seventy-two pack members. She seemed surprised when she saw how many there were, but she never faltered and tightened her grip on my hand. When we found the center, she stepped forward. I could feel her anxiety.

"Hello. My name is Juniper. I want to apologize for causing any of you any uncertainty. I have to say it came as a surprise to me as well. I want each of you to know that I wish no harm or bad will on anyone here. I have given up my entire family to be here when I felt my connection to For...I mean your Alpha. I would love to get to know each of you if you will let me."

My heart nearly burst with pride. She stood before them even after they had shouted and questioned her intentions. She reassured them, just as a Luna does. I thought I would protect her, keeping her from their judgments, but instead, she addressed it head-on. With the renewed assurances, we ended the meeting and left the way we had come.

"Welcome, Luna."

"We're so happy you're here."

Several people approached Juniper on our walk back to welcome her. I could feel her joy at the acceptance. Afterward, she took her time to thank each person. When we finally arrived home, I led her to the kitchen and started whipping up some dinner.

"I can't say that I'm a great cook, but I can handle a few things," I told her as I chopped the peppers and onions.

"Can I help?"

"Nope. You just sit there. You have gone above and beyond tonight."

She smiled at me and watched.

"Oh, Alpha. Forgive me for not preparing your dinner sooner. I was waiting until after the meeting," Joan, the house cook, said as she walked in the side door.

"Nothing to forgive," I smiled at her. "I would like to make my mate dinner tonight. Why don't you take the rest of the evening off?"

She lowered her head, "Thank you, Alpha."

We watched as she hurried off, and I added the meat to the sautéing vegetables.

"Hey, where did Poppy run off to? I'm famished," Oakley said when he rolled into the room.

"I sent her home, but we should have enough for you as well."

He held his hand to his chest, "You mean to tell me that the Alpha is making me dinner? I am honored."

He bowed his head in an amusing gesture.

"Knock that off if you want any."

"Of course," Oakley mused and sat next to Juniper on one of the stools at the counter.

"So, Luna. Tell me about yourself. Where do you hail from?"

"Like my home? The settlement I grew up in was in north-central Washington."

"Not a town?"

"We just call it the settlement. It's where my great-great-grand-mother and the other original five settled after they fled to America."

"What did they flee from?"

"Religious persecution," she shrugged as if everyone knew this story.

"Witch hunt, huh."

"Pretty much."

"What was life like back at your settlement?"

"We all worked together to make it work. It was nothing like your village. Simple, I guess I could describe it as. The elders educate the children until they turn sixteen. Once they come of age, they are assigned jobs. Mine was gathering and helping Heather, who was basically like an aunt to me. She makes products that she sells in town and online. It had become one of the main revenues for the coven."

"What type of products does she make?"

"Health and beauty products like lotions, shampoos, creams... What about you guys? Do you guys sell anything? How does your pack sustain itself?"

"We have quite a few resources for income. We have invest-ments, a copper mine, and a stake in an outdoor recreation store."

"Wow, really?"

"Yeah. Everyone in the pack either works with one of our busi-nesses or helps around the pack."

"No wonder you guys have a legit town."

Oakley laughed as I placed a couple of plates of stir-fry in front of them before walking around with my own and joining them at the counter. We continued talking while we enjoyed the meal. Watching the scene in front of me of my best friend and mate talking and joking together filled something inside of me. It felt good.

20

Juniper

After a few days hidden away in our apartment, Forest took me down to the town to get acquainted with it. There was both a diner and a cafe for food. We stopped at the cafe for a cup of tea. It was good, but I wanted to find some herbs to bring them and teach them how to make a real cup, one not made from store-bought sachets. Next, we went to a clothing store. I was impressed with how large of a variety it offered. Forest bought me a whole new wardrobe since I had been wearing his clothes the last few days. He sent the bags back to the house so we didn't need to tote them around while we wandered about. He pointed out a general store, grocery, and, of course, the clinic. There was even a fire department.

After we left the main street, he showed me the training fields. He explained that the pack had warrior wolves who patrolled and protected the pack. Each year, they held tryouts where anyone could compete to join the ranks. They currently had around seventy warriors. Even though these warriors trained daily, the rest of the pack was required to attend at least one class every week so that everyone had some basic knowledge of self-defense and fighting techniques.

Beyond the training fields were the farmlands. As we approached, Forest explained how they grew a handful of their food to help supplement their needs. Their grocers also ordered food from outside vendors. They even had a cattle ranch out back to help with meat, which I guess they ate a lot of.

"Look at all these!" I said excitedly when I spotted the herb garden.

I nearly ran over when I spotted it.

"I assume you like herbs?" Forest laughed as he followed me.

"Well, yeah. It goes with the whole witch thing," I teased him back.

I looked over the variety of plants growing. Most were the standard fare in a home garden. I picked a lavender stem and sniffed the fragrant flowers on the end.

"Would they mind if I planted a few more?"

"Not at all. You can do whatever you want out here. Oliver is in charge of the fields. I can take you over and introduce you to him."

"That would be great!"

"Do you want to go now?" He asked.

I think he had picked up on my excitement.

"Yes! Can we?" I said, jumping up and down.

He laughed hard and put an arm around my shoulder, "Sure thing."

We found Oliver checking on the cornfield. He lowered his head as we approached, something I was still getting used to. Forest told me it was a sign of respect for their Alpha and Luna. It goes back to their primal attributes, showing that they are submissive to their leaders. I didn't want anyone to be submissive to me. I would rather be treated equally, but I tried to understand that they had their own customs.

"Oliver, how are you?" Forest asked as we approached.

"I'm good. I'm just checking on the progress of the crops."

"How are they looking?"

"Good. I think we will have a fine yield this year."

"That's great. The Luna wondered if she could help in the herb garden?"

"Of course," he said. "It would be an honor to have her work with us."

"That would be wonderful, thank you. When can I start?" I asked excitedly.

He looked surprised.

"I head out first thing in the morning to tend to it. Would you like to join us tomorrow morning?"

"Yes! I will see you tomorrow, bright and early."

"See you tomorrow, Luna," he said with a smile.

We turned around, and I squeezed my fist to my cheeks in a fit of cute excitement. I was so happy to find something not only that I loved, but could be helpful with.

THE FOLLOWING MORNING, I was up before the sun, eager to head back to the gardens. I woke Forest as I scrambled in the bathroom, preparing for the day. I came out of the door in my towel, and a bit of steam followed me.

"That is a sight I could wake up to every morning," Forest said while still in bed.

I stopped and smiled at him.

"What, scattered-brain Juniper flying around?" I teased, referring to my frenzied state.

He stood from the bed and walked over to me, wrapping his strong arms around me and kissing my head.

"Mm, more like sultry Juniper emerging from a cloud of steam with nothing more than a small towel hiding her stunning body."

I bit my lip and blushed.

"Keep doing that, and I won't let you out of this room," he lusted at me.

"Okay, okay." I laughed. "You just keep it in your pants, so I'm not late."

He lay back down in the bed with a huff. I laughed at his man-sized tantrum as I ran into the closet and quickly dressed in a pair of faded jeans and a light blue button-up cotton shirt. I grabbed my Converse sneakers and a sun hat and checked myself in the mirror at the back of the door on my way out of the closet. Forest was sitting at the end of the bed, stretching out his neck. I skipped up to him, kissing his lips hard before heading out.

"Have fun," he called after me with laughter.

"Thanks, you too!"

I followed the roads down to the main street and grabbed a quick tea and a blueberry scone from the cafe we had stopped at yesterday before heading out of town toward the gardens. A picket fence welcomed me in as I walked under the arbor at the gate. A sea of green and light purple wisteria was cascading down the side of it. The strong smell of the flowers and herbs was like a welcoming embrace. Oliver was nowhere in sight, so I walked around, taking stock of the garden's contents.

"Good morning, Luna," Oliver said from behind me.

"Good morning."

"I see you've already made yourself at home," he smiled.

"I hope that's alright?" I asked with a smile.

"Sure is. I'm glad to have someone else so excited to be here. A few others will join us in a bit. They help with weeding, harvesting, and storing the crops."

"Great. What can I do?"

"Let me show you around first."

I followed him down the aisles as he told me what was in each bed. It soon turned from herbs to rows of vegetables and berry patches. Past a row of hedges, the area opened to a sea of colorful flowers. Every color of the rainbow was present.

"I didn't know you grew flowers! What are they for?"

"It's a small flower farm. We use them for decorating the community buildings and pack events, and the grocer sells them in their shop for people to buy."

"It's stunning."

He showed me a shed they used to house tools and baskets as we walked back near the vegetables.

"We need to pinch the basil. Those buggers are quick to flower on me. After that, you can gather any ripened strawberries from the patch over yonder," He directed with his hand.

"No problem. Where would you like me to take them when I'm done?"

"I'll bring my truck over and park it near the gate. Just set them in there. I deliver them to the grocers and pack house."

I nodded and thanked him before he turned to leave. I made my way over to the basil and knelt down, pinching the small budding blooms from each one and saving the tiny leaves attached. Being back in a garden and working with plants made me feel at home. I had missed this, my hands covered in dirt and the smell of earth sticking to my clothes. Though it brought me happiness, it also brought a sense of homesickness. A remembrance of the life I had left behind, but as I searched within myself, I could feel my connection with Forest. I was reminded of the warmth that this new adventure brought to me.

I LOADED the last baskets of strawberries into the old rusty blue pickup truck and turned to Oliver.

"Thank you for letting me help out today."

"Any time. I'm happy for the help."

"So... every day?"

He held his belly and laughed, "Absolutely."

We said our goodbyes, and I walked back up the gravel road and into town. The street was bustling with people. Children ran around laughing, chasing each other, and playing various games. I even spotted a few playing tricks on some poor passerby. There was so much life and energy here. You would never have guessed that the whole town was comprised of shifters. I caught sight of the diner up on the corner, and as if on cue, my stomach growled in hunger.

Are you up for lunch? I mind-linked Forest, thinking maybe he could meet me there.

I can't. I'm sorry. I'm running the north border right now. How about dinner tonight?

Sounds great. See you then.

I pursed my lips as I debated whether to go home and whip up my own lunch or head to the diner and eat there. With another growl of my stomach and the mouth-watering aroma sifting through the air from the building up ahead, the decision almost seemed to be made for me. A bell chimed as I walked through the door. Everyone in the packed restaurant turned to look at me, making me freeze. I waved my hand slightly, unsure what I should be doing at that moment.

"Luna, how can we help you?" a middle-aged woman with Rose displayed on her name tag asked as she approached.

"Um, I was hoping to grab some lunch."

"Of course. Let me clear the table for you."

She walked to a booth near a window and talked to the people sitting there. They all started grabbing their plates to stand. I quickly walked over.

"Oh, please don't do that. I can wait for a spot to open up."

I noticed everyone was still watching me, setting my nerves on end.

"Really, I insist. Let them eat," I smiled at them.

They sat back down, smiling back at me.

"Thank you, Luna," they both said.

"I'm finished here." Another man offered from the stool at the counter. "Please have my spot, Luna."

Rose rushed over and cleared his plate away.

"Are you sure? I don't want to chase you away from your lunch."

"Oh, I'm quite stuffed and need to head back to work."

"Thank you. I appreciate it."

He smiled at me while bowing his head slightly and headed out. I took his seat and noticed that everyone seemed to have gotten back to their food. Rose wiped down the counter in front of me.

"What can I get you to drink, Luna?"

"Iced tea would be great."

"Of course."

She headed off to fill my drink, giving me a moment to take in what had just happened. I didn't want anyone to treat me above anyone else, yet they all seemed to go out of their way to accommodate me. I would have to show them there was no need to do so. Rose returned with my iced tea and a menu, setting them before me. The glistening condensation on the outside of the glass was an addictive call to satisfy my thirst. I picked it up and took a large sip.

"Just what I needed. Thank you," I smiled up at Rose.

She stood and watched as I browsed over their selection. I figured she had other stuff to do, but I didn't want her to think I was shooing her off, so I smiled at her again before looking back at the menu. There was a selection of sandwiches, burgers, soups, and salads, along with some more hearty options such as steak and chicken.

"Can I have a garden salad with some vinaigrette, please?"

"Of course, and what else?"

"That's all."

"I'll have it right out for you."

I was finally able to take in the place around me. It was right out of the pages of a 1950s book. Bright red upholstered booths ran the length of the exterior wall, as well as a row in the center of the room. An extended counter lined with stools sat against the interior wall. On the opposite side of the counter were a few drink machines, a set of double swinging doors, and a window that looked into the kitchen. There was even a jukebox that sat in the corner, blaring old music. Every seat in the diner was filled, and the chatter of their conversations hummed throughout the space.

"Hi," I said awkwardly as I smiled at the people on either side of me.

They each lowered their head, "Luna."

"What's your name?" I asked the girl to my right.

"Fawn."

"Nice to meet you."

Right as she went to reply, the bell on the door rang, and I looked over. The room quieted down to a deafening silence. A tall, attractive woman with shoulder-length blonde hair walked in confidently. Rose walked around the counter and approached her.

"Good afternoon. There will be a bit of a wait, I'm afraid."

The woman scoffed at her as if she were just insulted.

"That's unacceptable. I'm sure you can boot someone out for me."

My jaw nearly dropped at her audacious attitude. No wonder they tried to do the same for me if someone like her demanded such catering upon her arrival. Who was she anyway? I hadn't seen anyone else act so entitled in my few days here.

"Sorry, but no. You will just have to wait. I'm sure it won't be long."

"How dare you treat me this way! I have never had to wait for a seat here before. You'd better sort this out, or I will sort you out, Rose."

I quickly stood up with a confidence I didn't know I had. "Leave her alone. You are just going to have to wait or leave."

Her eyes quickly landed on one.

"Oh, look who it is. The Alpha's little whore witch who caught him in one of her spells."

I was shocked.

"I'm sorry if that is what you think about me, but I didn't cast any spell. It just happened," I said, defending myself.

"Is that what you're going with? We all know that a wolf won't mate with anyone but another wolf. And you're saying you mated with the most powerful Alpha in North America? A witch...sure, we all know that you did something to him, and I will be sure to squash out whatever magic you used and take my place back at his side."

His side? Is this the woman Forest had told me about? What was her name? That's right...Sienna. I could feel my anger surge.

"Listen here, I was just as surprised as he was to realize we are mates. There's no magic, no spell, just whatever bond or pull or whatever you want to describe it as. You can accept it or leave me be. But I won't be talked to that way."

"And what are you going to do? Cast a spell on me, too? Do you hear that?" she said to the room, "She's going to put some evil little spell of hers on me. She needs to be taken out before she imprisons us all in her web of lies!"

The sound of whispers began to chirp like crickets in the evening. The door behind her swung open, and two large men walked in, grabbing hold of her arms.

"Let go of me!" she screamed. "Do you see what she is doing?

She probably called them using some kind of magic and is making them drag me away. She's a witch! She can't be trusted."

As they pulled her back through the doors, August walked in, looking around the room.

"That woman is crazy," he said before approaching me.

"Are you alright, Luna?" he asked me.

I felt like I was rooted to the spot. My mind was racing, trying to comprehend what had just happened. I rubbed my forehead with one hand.

"What the hell was that?" I asked him.

"That was Sienna. The most entitled psychopath you will ever meet."

"You can say that again. Is that the girl Forest told me about?"

"Yup," he said, popping the 'p'. "She's just mad that she doesn't hold any clout around the pack anymore."

"So she throws me under the bus because I'm a witch? Is that what everyone thinks of me?" I nearly whispered the last part.

"No," he said confidently. "I trust you, and I know that your bond is real. I see it."

"Thank you," I sighed as Rose set my salad in front of me with a sympathetic smile.

I looked around the room and noticed all the stolen glances in my direction. My appetite had left at the same time Sienna did. I looked at the piled lettuce and vegetables in front of me and slid it away.

"I'm not so hungry anymore. I think I will head home."

I stood up from the stool and tossed some of the money Forest had given me on the counter. I didn't even bother counting. Hopefully, it was enough to cover my bill.

"I'll walk back with you," August offered.

I forced a smile at him as we left.

21

Forest

I was happy to see Juniper throwing herself into helping the pack. Her excitement only fueled my own. Part of pack life was working together. Everyone helped out in one way or another. We compensated everyone for their work, knowing that most of it returned to the pack. However, some would spend their money through online stores to get clothes and other items that our little town didn't sell. The town itself was its own economy. Of course, we made sure everyone was taken care of. As our elders aged and could no longer work, the pack cared for their needs. Those who could not work for one reason or another were supplemented appropriately. Everyone had full access to food and basic needs whether they could afford it or not.

Since Juniper would be busy most of the morning, I decided I needed to catch up on some work. I grabbed a quick shower and headed down to my office to find a pile of papers that had collected over the last few days while we hid in our apartment. I sighed and plopped down in my chair, grabbing the first off of the stack.

Oakley strolled in, leaning on my door frame. "Back to work already?"

"Unfortunately..."

"Are you ready for a rundown, or do you need some time?" He asked.

"Lay it on me."

He walked into the room and sat on the opposite side of my desk.

"Alpha Luke from the Sea Wind Pack called. He wanted to set up a gathering between our two packs. They hope some of their members may find mates with us."

"Alright, I will give him a call. What else?"

"The patrol picked up a rogue scent last night on our northern border. I was going to head up and take a look."

I stopped and looked up at him. "You didn't think to start with that?"

"Lark said they only picked up one scent, and it led away from the pack. Probably just a wandering rogue who got too close to our border."

"You know you are supposed to inform me immediately if patrols pick up the scent of rogues."

"You said not to bother you while you got better acquainted with Juniper," he smirked.

"Oakley, I swear, " I threatened him, causing his grin to grow. I took a deep breath to stop myself from strangling him. "Next time, let me know right away."

"Of course, Alpha."

I stood up, "I'm going to go check the border. Have Lark meet me out there."

"Will do. Do you want me to come?"

"Yeah, seems like you still need some training," I teased.

Oakley sighed and followed after me.

WE HAD BEEN RUNNING the border for several hours. When I caught the rogue's scent that Lark had found, I followed it off our lands for a few miles. It seemed that Lark's assessment had been correct, as it had remained a single scent, and the rogue continued in the opposite direction from our pack as far as I trailed him. I wanted to be sure there were no others and that he hadn't made another go at our territory, so I decided to run the rest of our northern border. I sent Oakley in the other direction so that we could cover twice the distance.

Are you up for lunch? Juniper linked me.

I can't, I'm sorry. I'm running the north border right now. How about dinner tonight?

Sounds great. See you then.

I was mad at myself. I had wanted to be there when Juniper finished. I had hoped that it went well and she enjoyed herself. If not for this damn rogue, I would have been sitting in my office and would have welcomed a break with her. The best I could do now was try and wrap up here so I could get back to her quickly. I pushed forward, following the trail around our territory. I could feel Juniper get nervous about something. I thought about mind-linking her, but I didn't want her to feel like I was intruding on her thoughts. After five minutes, her emotions subsided to more of an uncomfortable feeling, easing my worry.

I jumped over a large log, landing near the river's rushing waters, when I felt a surge of anger swell inside me. Juniper...what would she be angry at? I thought about running to her when I pulled myself back. I had never had to navigate someone else's feelings before, especially someone that every instinct I had told me to protect. If I ran to her every time she had a strong emotion, we would be inseparable. I continued, trotting up the riverbank.

Alpha, there is a problem at the diner. Cane, one of my warriors, linked me.

I halted, waiting to see if I needed to return to town. *What is it?*

Sienna is in the diner screaming at the Luna.

I could feel my hackles rise at the threat to my mate. August had told me to expect something from her, but I was stupid enough to think she wouldn't try anything. Of course, she would. I turned and raced back in the direction of town.

Get Sienna out of there now! Hold her in a cell.

Yes, Alpha

August, get to the diner now. Sienna is yelling at Juniper. I linked to him.

On it, Alpha, he replied.

Juniper's feelings turned to sadness. My heart ached for her.

I have the Luna. We are heading back to the pack house, A few minutes later, August linked me back.

Stay with her until I get there.

Yes, Alpha.

I ran to the back door of the pack house and shifted, not even wasting time, to redress before racing up the stairs. August was standing outside our apartment doors.

"She said she wanted to be alone, so I waited out here."

I nodded at him and opened the door, heading in. I looked across the room, finding it empty. Walking down the hall, I found the bedroom doors closed. I peeked inside and saw a lump under the covers on the bed. I could hear Juniper's sniffles from within. I walked over and sat on the edge of the bed, rubbing her back through the covers.

"What happened?" I asked her in a calm, quiet voice.

I wanted to be comforting, even though my anger at Sienna was burning within me. Her cries grew louder. I slipped under the covers and wrapped my body around hers. She turned and tucked her head against my chest, wrapping her arms around me. I let her cry as long as she needed. After several minutes, she pulled her head out of the covers. Her eyes were red and swollen, and her face was soaked from all of her tears. I wiped away the wetness with my thumb as I held her cheek.

"Can you tell me what happened?"

"D-does everyone think I put you under some love spell or something?"

"What? Of course not. Is that what Sienna said?"

"She told me that the only way I could have mated with you was through magic. She said wolves only mate with other wolves. Is that true?"

I sighed heavily, "Obviously not...I'm mated with you. But," I hesitated, "I have never known any others to mate outside of our species."

"T-then, why did we mate together?"

"Because the moon goddess decided to pair us. She has her reasons. We have to trust in her."

She curled back into me and started crying again. I felt helpless at that moment. I had wondered how the pack would take having a witch as their Luna, but we had never been on bad terms with witches before. I figured that they would learn to accept her over time, but if that bitch, Sienna, is off running her mouth and turning my pack against their Luna, I needed to put a stop to it before it gained any footing. Juniper's breathing evened out, and I could tell she had drifted off to sleep. I slipped out from underneath her and grabbed some clothes.

I want to talk to everyone who was at the diner when Sienna was there, I linked Oakley and August.

Yes, Alpha, they both replied.

I headed down to my office and sat at my desk. It took everything in me not to go down to the cells and rip Sienna apart for hurting Juniper, but I needed to be diplomatic about how I handled this situation. While Sienna is a pain, she is a pack member and was with me for the last several years, imposing herself in the Luna role more than I ever cared for. I needed to be sure she didn't have a following that may rebel against her punishment. I also needed to know the whole picture so I could adequately decide exactly what I would do with her. I couldn't kill her for harsh words, but I could severely punish her. There was a knock at my door.

"Come in," I called out.

"Alpha," Rose, the diner's head waitress, said as she opened the door slowly, her head bowed.

"Rose, take a seat."

She walked over and sat in a chair across from my desk.

"I'm sure you know why I have called you here. Please tell me about the events at the diner today involving the Luna."

"Uh, she came in at the lunch rush. There were no tables. I asked Landon if his table could be cleared out for her, but she stopped us. She told us she could wait for a seat."

A smile crept across my face at that information.

Rose continued, "Sol offered up his seat at the counter since he had just finished. She ordered a garden salad, and Sienna came in only a few minutes later. She made a whole stink about wanting a table. I told her that she would have to wait. She was livid and threatened me. The Luna stood and told her to stop. Sienna called her..."

She was hesitant, not wanting to repeat whatever Sienna called her.

"Go ahead, I want every detail."

"She called the Luna your whore."

A low growl ripped from my throat. Rose looked terrified, and I fought to reel myself in. I had not intended to scare her, but the insult to Juniper stoked my wolf's instinct to defend her.

"Continue..." I gritted my teeth.

With her head lowered, she continued, "S-she went on a-about how the Luna must have cast a spell on you. The Luna denied it, and when the Luna told h-her not to talk to her in such a way, S-sienna implied that the Luna would cast a spell on her and that s-she needed to b-be taken out."

The wood on the arms of my chair splintered within my hands, and a low growl ripped from within me. I could feel my wolf close to the surface, and I'm sure my eyes were as black as onyx. My deep, jagged breaths echoed in the otherwise quiet room. There was a knock on the door, and Oakley peeked his head in.

"Is everything alright?" he asked.

He could see poor Rose terrified, sitting across from me, and stepped into the room, closing the door behind him.

"Thank you, Rose, you may leave."

"Y-yes, Beta," she stuttered before scurrying out the door.

Oakley watched as she softly shut the door behind her and sat across from me.

"Do you want me to send the others away?"

"No..." I took several deep breaths, fighting to control my temper. "I want you and August to interview them. Decide what everyone's opinion is of the event. Do they share the same beliefs as Sienna? Did she influence them?"

"Yeah, I gotcha, Alpha."

I stormed out of my office once he left. I had never had such a loose grip on my control before, but anytime I felt a threat against Juniper or my relationship with her, it was as if the rug was pulled out from under me. I needed to get a grasp on this before I did something I regretted. For now, I needed to be close to Juniper, to my mate. I entered our bedroom to find the bed empty. My wolf, who was already on edge, began to panic.

"Juniper!" I called out.

"In the bath," she yelled back from the bathroom.

I entered the room and found her goddess-like body soaking in the steamy water. I stripped down and climbed in behind her, pulling her to my chest and inhaling her scent. She rubbed my arms, which were tightly wrapped around her.

"Is everything alright, Forest? I could feel your anger."

"I just need to be close to you. The whole thing with Sienna at the diner is getting to me. She should know better than to act like that."

She turned her torso to face me and cupped my face, inspecting my sour expression. She leaned forward, lightly kissing my lips. The rest of the world melted away and became just the two of us. I pulled her tightly to me, probing her lips with my tongue, asking for entry. Her lips parted, and I swirled my tongue around hers, deepening the kiss. I'm sure she could feel me harden against her.

A small moan escaped her lips, driving me wild. My hands roamed her back, savoring every inch of her silky skin. I lifted her, turning her so that she straddled me. Water splashed up against the tub's sides, splattering to the ground. She lowered herself down on my stiff shaft. Both of us moaned from the sensation.

"Fuck, Juniper...you feel so damn good," I huffed out as she began rocking on me.

Her breathing hastened, and she leaned her head on my shoulder. She sped her pace up, sending waves crashing across our bodies. I could hear the sound of water pooling on the floor around us. Her breath hitched as I felt her tighten her core around me, her whole body tensing as she rode out her orgasm. I kept up the pace, lifting her and thrusting in rhythm so that I could drag it out as long as possible.

Once I felt her muscles release, and her breath returned to her, I slowly pulled out and turned her around again so that she was on her knees, grabbing ahold of the edge of the bathtub. I slammed back into her. She screamed out and rolled her head in ecstasy.

"Forest... more, I need more," she moaned out.

I was happy to oblige, grabbing firmly onto her hips and increasing my momentum. Over and over, I pushed myself as deeply as I could into her. I could feel myself swell, and with one last hard thrust, I felt her come once more as I filled her, pumping a few more times to finish us both off. I leaned down and kissed up her spine, watching the goosebumps form alongside my lips. I finally felt relaxed. She was truly the perfect medicine.

22

Juniper

I returned to the gardens the following morning. Though I was nervous venturing out of the pack house, I felt like I needed to go out and show Sienna that she couldn't scare me away. When I arrived, Oliver was already working in the vegetable patch and welcomed me with a sympathetic smile. He obviously knew what had transpired at the diner yesterday. The whole pack probably did. What do they all think of me?

Sensing my unease, he spoke up as we walked toward the garden shed, "May I speak freely, Luna?"

"Of course," I replied.

"I wouldn't take Sienna's words to heart. As the saying goes, there are always a few bad apples in every barrel, and I would say she is one of them."

I stopped, turning to look at him, "Why would you say that?"

"She has been known to lash out at others. For some unknown reason, she feels she is better than the rest of the pack and makes it a point to tell everyone. No one here will take her word to heart, and neither should you," he said firmly but gently.

"Thank you, Oliver," I gently smiled at him.

His words helped ease some of the tension building inside me. If Oliver hadn't judged me on my origins and had not been influenced by Sienna's rant, then, by Selene's grace, others wouldn't have been either.

After our morning talk, Oliver had me pull carrots and cut lettuce heads for the day, allowing me to lose myself in the earth. After finishing my tasks, I carried the crops to his truck parked near the gate and found Forest leaning against it, smiling at me.

"What are you doing here?" I asked, surprised.

"Thought we could go grab some lunch," he answered as he pushed himself off the truck.

I bit my lip, and my nerves turned over. Going to the gardens and walking through the town was one thing, but how could I face everyone from yesterday? She basically tried to start a witch hunt against me. How many of those people were her friends? Would they do the same? Would they demand my death as had happened to my ancestors before me?

"At the house?" I pleadingly asked.

I figured I could persuade him to head back to the pack house. That way, I could avoid any confrontation.

"We could, but I was thinking of the diner."

"Are you sure that's a good idea? After yesterday, I'm not sure anyone wants me there."

"That's not true. You stood up to a bully. You showed the pack that you are strong and a good leader, standing up for them when someone treats them poorly."

Is that what they honestly thought? I took a deep breath in, trying to build up my courage.

"Okay," I said, more uncertain than I had hoped to.

He took hold of my hand and led me up the road to the town.

There were a handful of people out and about. I noticed them looking our way, but they never stared. I wasn't sure how to take that. As we walked into the diner, it was just as packed as yesterday. I noticed several people whom I recognized from my last visit.

Rose walked up to us with a beaming smile.

"Alpha," she nodded her head at Forest before looking at me. "Luna, I wanted to thank you for yesterday."

"I...um, for what?" I asked, surprised.

"For telling Sienna not to talk to me that way. She has always been difficult, and I'm glad someone has put her in her place. I'm just sorry she turned that foul mouth of hers on you."

"Thank you," I replied, realizing the importance of what Forest had told me.

I looked around the diner and realized everyone was watching our interaction. Most of them nodded and smiled at me in agreement with Rose's testament. Forest wrapped his arm around my waist, pulling me closer. I could feel his pride in me, filling me with warmth.

"Anyhow, I have a table for you two over here," she directed us to the far corner by the window.

A couple stood up and vacated the seats.

"Rose, no one needs to leave. We can wait for a table." I insisted.

"Thank you, Luna," the woman smiled at me, "but we are all done here. Please have it."

"Okay, I don't want to rush you out," I offered.

"Not at all," she assured me.

Forest and I sat down across from each other. Rose returned a moment later with menus and two glasses of water.

"Do you two need some time, or are you ready to order?"

Forest looked over at me as I peeked at the menu.

"Are you ready?" I asked him.

"Sure am, go ahead," he grinned.

"I'll have iced tea and a garden salad, please."

"Would you like the vinaigrette again or something else?"

"The vinaigrette's fine, thank you."

She smiled at me and turned to Forest.

"And for you, Alpha?"

"I'll have a coffee and my usual steak."

"I'll have it right out for you."

I peered across the room, noticing the lack of stares. Maybe it really was only Sienna's opinion. I felt a wave of reassurance and relaxed into my seat. The whole meal after that was enjoyable. The fresh produce they had used made a light and refreshing salad. It was loaded with tomatoes, cucumbers, peppers, shaved carrots, and peas. Forest had a massive steak. I couldn't believe that he could eat all of it. One thing I had learned since arriving here was that shifters ate a lot. Forest explained that it was due to their fast metabolism.

"Would you like to help me with some pack business today?" Forest asked as we exited the diner.

"Really?" I replied excitedly.

"Yeah," he smiled at me. "I check in with the shops once a month. They turn in any orders they need and the financial statements. I also like checking in on them personally to see if they need anything."

"Where do we start?"

"Let's head to Aspen's," he answered, gesturing down the street.

"The clothing store?"

I remembered it from when he had taken me shopping on my second day here. We walked into the posh shop that had racks of clothing lining the walls and several displays in the center. The crisp white walls with golden accents made it feel like a luxury shop, while pricing kept it accessible to everyone. Aspen, the proprietor, had a good variety of pieces to accommodate everyone's tastes. There were jeans, skirts, all sorts of shirts, and dresses. We walked up to the counter made with actual aspen trees displaying their trademark bark.

"Hello, Alpha, Luna," A young brunette said from the register.

"Hey, Aspen, we are checking in for the month."

"Of course," she dug under the counter, pulling out a manila file folder. "Here are my reports. It's been a busy month. A lot of people have been buying clothes for summer."

"That's good. Do you need to do any orders?"

"Yeah, I would like to get some more swimwear in, and I had a few specific requests."

"Go ahead and order them, and let us know what day the order will arrive."

"Thank you, Alpha."

She smiled at both of us before we left.

Once outside, I asked him, "Do they have to get approval for all their orders?"

"We just want to know if humans will be coming into town. We also help cover some of the costs to make it more affordable for our pack members."

I nodded in understanding. We went through each business along the main street. It was nice to meet so many people on a more personal basis. We stopped a little longer to talk to a few, while others were busy and could only chat for a second to hand over their reports. We returned home, and Forest went to work to make dinner for us. I sat on the stool across the counter and talked to him. Once we were done eating, we sat on the couch in our apartment. I could feel his mood shift as he turned towards me with a serious look.

"What's wrong?" I asked, worried.

"Tomorrow, I will be punishing Sienna."

"For what?"

"For how she behaved in the diner."

"Oh..." I said somberly.

"Wolves have strict laws that they abide by in their packs. No one can disrespect any high-ranking wolf. It can be considered a challenge, which is what she did with you."

"How is it normally handled?" I asked, concerned.

"Depends...Anyone can challenge the Alpha for his position. It is a fight to the death."

My eyes widened in disbelief.

"We solve most of our disputes with physical challenges. It is a way of showing our strength. If someone disrespects the Luna, they are either cast out from the pack or ordered to do hard physical labor for a year. If they threaten the Luna, they are killed."

That all seemed extreme. While I was unhappy about the incident, I did not think it warranted banishment or death.

"W-what are you going to do to her?" I asked nervously.

"She threatened you. It was ridiculously stupid of her. She knew what she was doing."

"You can't kill her," I said aghastly.

"I have to. If I don't, it goes against our customs and hierarchy. It would show weakness not only in my role as Alpha but for your position as Luna."

"No," I said firmly. "I cannot condone you killing her. She was a pain, but you cannot kill someone for hateful words alone."

He sighed heavily, "Then what do you think we should do?"

"Give her a year of labor. She just needs to be taught a lesson. She went from being by your side to being replaced by an outsider. Give her a chance to prove herself before condemning her."

He ran his hand back through his hair, "I would like you there when I announce it."

"Okay. If you promise not to kill her."

"As long as she doesn't pull anything stupid, I promise."

23

Forest

I woke early in the morning and snuck out of bed to avoid waking Juniper. My least favorite part of my job was disciplining my pack members. Even though Sienna deserved much worse than what she would be receiving, I knew she would throw a fit about being tasked with hard labor. She had refused to clean up after herself when she stayed over, always saying there were people for that kind of work. Now that I had been with Juniper, I couldn't fathom what I had seen in her. Juniper was kind, caring, and considerate of those around her, never wanting to hinder others, while Sienna demanded that the world bow to her every need. I wished I had never let things get as far as they had with her.

After a quick shower, I headed down to my office to review all the business reports we had picked up yesterday. After an hour or so, Juniper came and found me. She walked around my desk and sat in my lap, kissing me quickly.

"What are you doing up so early?" she asked.

"I'm trying to finish some work ahead of the day."

She bit her lip and nodded. I knew she could feel my uneasiness about the day ahead, but she said nothing more.

"Have you eaten breakfast yet?"

"Nope. Would you like to grab some with me?"

"Yeah, I make a mean pancake," she offered as she stood before pulling me up.

"Sounds great," I chuckled.

Breakfast with Juniper was precisely what I needed to calm the growing anticipation inside me. After breakfast, she headed to the gardens to work, and I settled back at my desk. Sienna's sentencing was set for this afternoon. I just needed to keep myself busy until then. By lunch, I stood to meet with Juniper and take her to the diner. I felt that it was vital for her to make herself known after the whole Sienna event, which meant we would eat there almost every day for the next few weeks. I was proud of her for going back yesterday. I could feel how nervous she had been. As I opened the door, I was faced with Cliff and Opal, Sienna's parents.

"Alpha, we were hoping to speak with you for a moment," Cliff said respectfully, but I caught a slight hint of desperation.

"Come in," I held the door open, gesturing them in.

"Thank you, Alpha," Opal said, walking past me.

I already knew why they were there; in fact, I was surprised it had taken them so long to show up at my door. Even with my mind made up on Sienna's punishment, I still needed to hear them out. They had always coddled Sienna. She was their only child, and they gave in to every single whim and request she sent their way. They had always thrown her lavish birthday parties and bought her all the new clothes that came in. Spoiled was an understatement.

"What can I do for you two?" I asked in a professional tone.

"I'm sure you know why we are here," Cliff started, "We were hoping that with your history with Sienna, you would grant her some leniency. She is hurting from losing you. We're sure she didn't mean anything she said about the Luna."

"She seemed serious enough to try and rally the entire diner to, and I quote, 'take her out.'"

"Alpha, please. She's a good girl. Sometimes her words just get ahead of her," Opal begged.

"If it were up to me, death would be her consequence."

"No, Alpha. S-she's a good girl. She has done so much for you. She's in love with you, don't you see that?" Opal interrupted.

"Do not interrupt me," I said sternly and stared them down.

They both dropped their heads.

"As I was saying, if it were up to me, she would be put to death. However, my mate, the rightful Luna of our pack, has deemed that too harsh a punishment. You both will accept her punishment when the time comes. It will be announced at her sentencing this afternoon." I softened my tone, "Trust in your Luna. She is a good woman."

"Thank you, Alpha," Cliff said, bowing his head before pulling a sobbing Opal out of her chair.

I leaned back in my chair and pinched the bridge of my nose after they had left. I understood where they were coming from; after all, she was their daughter. Any parent would beg for their child's life, but she was still guilty. They needed to accept her for who she was and the actions she committed. I peeked at the clock and realized that I would be late picking up Juniper. Hopefully, I could still catch her on her walk back.

I had just walked out of the pack house when Oakley linked me, *Alpha. We need you on the south border.*

What's going on?

An elderly woman is calling the Luna's name from the trail close to the Harper cabin, he reported.

On my way.

I wanted to check out this woman discreetly. I was concerned that it was Juniper's family coming to try and take her back. I wasn't sure how far they were willing to take things after having cast some spell on her to control her. I grabbed a bag inside with some spare clothes before making my way back out and stripping. I shifted into my wolf and raced around the town, heading to the familiar area. When I found Oakley, he was crouched in some bushes on a small ridge around thirty meters on the other side of the creek where I had first seen Juniper.

"Juniper..." An elderly voice called with desperation.

How long has she been out here? I linked Oakley.

It has been a few hours. She has made her way up and down the trail a few times and even wandered into the woods.

I slowly moved forward, finding a slender woman with long silver hair resting on a rock. Deep bags were underneath her eyes, and her face was plastered with concern. After several minutes, she pushed herself back up and called for Juniper again. This had to be her family.

Have you seen any others? I asked Oakley.

No.

I'm going to talk to her. Watch my back.

Are you sure?

Yes.

I dropped the bag of clothes I had brought and shifted, changing into them before walking over to her. When I emerged from the dense forest, her eyes widened, but she said nothing.

"Why are you calling Juniper?"

"I am looking for my granddaughter. She went missing around here the week before last."

"What do you want with Juniper?"

Her already wide eyes turned to saucers.

"Are you the one who took her?" she asked accusingly.

"No one took her. She came with us," I challenged back.

"She wouldn't leave me."

"She found her mate in our pack.

She looked like she was momentarily lost in thought, "Can you take me to her? Please, I need to see her. I need to make sure she is alright."

"How do we know that you will not force her back?" I demand.

She scoffs before saying, "No one can force Juniper to do anything."

"They can when they cast some control spell on her," I reply accusingly.

Her eyes widened in surprise for a brief moment before she hardened her features again and said, "No one would do that. Those types of spells have been banned for decades."

"Then why did we have to rescue her from a woman who had cast one on her?"

This time, her stunned face stayed in place when she asked, "What? Who?"

"Someone named Heather," I replied, unwilling to back down. I could tell she was surprised, but that did not lessen the offense done onto Juniper.

"Heather...she wouldn't..." Her voice trailed off.

"She would, and did. She forced Juniper to leave with her. We stopped her after she called out for help."

"If she were under the spell, she wouldn't have been able to call for help," she attempted to argue.

"She could to her mate," I challenge.

"Telepathy? I have heard wolves could speak telepathically to one another, but..." she stopped and looked at me. "Please, let me just talk to her."

"Go to the cabin. I will bring her tomorrow if she is willing to come."

"Are you her mate?" she asked me before I could turn to leave.

"Yes."

I disappeared into the forest's overgrowth, returning to the bag

I had left hidden in the shrubs. After stripping once more, I shifted and ran back towards Oakley.

I want eyes on her and the cabin. If you see any others, report to me immediately.

Yes, Alpha.

Now, I needed to figure out how to tell Juniper about this while dealing with the Sienna situation.

24

Juniper

I had hoped Forest would meet me after my work in the gardens this morning, but when I saw no sign of him, I decided to head back to the pack house and make myself a sandwich. August joined me once I arrived. It was nice to get to know him better. He was a year older than Forest, and along with Oakley, they had been best friends since childhood. His father was the Gamma before him and still lives in town with his mother and younger sister.

I cleaned up from lunch, even though Joan, the house cook, protested. She was a wonderful grandmotherly woman who constantly insisted on making me food and treats. I grabbed a book from the library and wandered onto the front porch, cozying on an oversized cushion lounge chair. Joan came out with a hot cup of tea and a plate of cookies, placing them on the table beside me.

"Thank you, Joan," I said, smirking at her stubbornness.

"You're welcome, Luna," she smiled triumphantly back at me.

I sat up and sipped on the herbal lavender tea. Over the last few days, she had worked hard to learn how I liked things. I was impressed with how spot-on she had become. I scrunched up my shoulders at the familiar comfort and breathed in the hot, humid steam. When I opened my eyes, I spotted Forest's familiar wolf jogging from the side of the house. His large paws trudged up the steps and stopped before me, dropping a bag on the ground before shifting. My eyes took in his tall, muscular figure in front of me, and I felt tingles leading down my spine, bringing warmth to my core. He smirked at me.

"Not here, little mate."

"What? I wasn't."

"Yeah, you were," he laughed, opening the bag and pulling out a pile of clothes.

I watched his muscles flex as he dressed himself and sat beside me.

"Are you ready for this afternoon?" He asked.

My stomach twisted, remembering Sienna's sentencing.

"I think I'm as ready as I will ever be. How long do we have before we have to go?"

"About twenty minutes."

He reached over and grabbed a cookie off the plate on the table.

"How can you be so casual about it right now?" I asked, baffled.

"Honestly, you pardoning her to a year's worth of work versus death is pretty forgiving, though I want you to be prepared for her not to take it well. She has been known to be a bit...over-dramatic."

"You think? That's why she is in this mess. I would be fine with no punishment. It's not like she physically attacked me."

"She disrespected you," he said seriously. "In our culture, that is just as bad."

I sighed, understanding what he meant. He took my hand and rubbed small circles on the back of it, trying to comfort me.

"I'm going to shower quickly, and then we will go."

"Okay..."

He stood and kissed my forehead, and ran into the house. I took another long sip of my tea, willing it to bring me the peace I craved so desperately.

WE STOOD on a stage set up on one of the training grounds. A large crowd had gathered in front of us, and waves of murmurs could be heard from them. Forest held my hand, giving it a little squeeze and snapping me out of my head. He stepped forward, projecting his voice as he talked.

"Bring forth the accused," he called.

The doors to a building to the right of the stage flew open, and two men dragged out a grungy Sienna. Her clothes were torn, and her face was covered in dirt and filth. I looked over at Forest, wishing he would explain why she looked in such disrepair, but his eyes never left the crowd. They stopped in front of the stage, turning her to face us. She scowled at me, her eyes filled with hatred. I hoped my leniency would help her, but I was second-guessing that hope with how she acted even now.

"West Moon Pack, Sienna Ridge has been found guilty of insulting and threatening the Luna. Under our laws, she should be sentenced to death."

I could hear sobbing coming from my side. I turned to find the source and spotted an older couple holding each other. Were those her parents? They must have been based on their display of emotion. Glancing across the sea of people, I saw no other tears, no longing on anyone's face. It was as if they had already accepted her death, or was she just that disliked?

Forest continued, pulling me from my thoughts, "However, your Luna has stepped in on her behalf and asked for a lesser punishment."

I could hear a few gasps, surprising me.

"She has asked that instead of death, Sienna Ridge be tasked with one year of hard labor. As I'm sure you all know, that will entail living out of the barracks and working to maintain our roads and agricultural land with no pay. Her funds will be stripped, and she will be provided only the essentials until her time has been served, in which case the pack will welcome her back."

There seemed to be more angry than happy faces in the crowd at Forest's announcement. Maybe I overstepped... Should we have banished her? Or even, dare I say it, killed her? It all seemed too dramatic for a bit of yelling in the diner. I looked over at her parents, who were smiling and crying what I believed were tears of joy. At least I could protect them from a little heartache. Sienna screamed in front of us, snapping my attention back to her.

"No! I will not do it! Every one of you is crazy if you do not see what that witch is doing to our Alpha! There is no way he would choose her over me. She's not even a wolf. It's unnatural. I gave up everything for you, and you just tossed me aside. You will pay for this!"

Growls ripped through the crowd. I was sure their hackles would be showing if they were in their wolf forms. Forest pulled me behind him and stepped forward.

"You insult your Luna again and threaten me? Your stupidity has got the best of you once more. Even though Luna has asked for leniency, your actions today have shown that even then, you will not change. I sentence you to death!"

Suddenly, an explosion rippled from the back of the crowd. Forest dropped me to the ground, covering me with his body as chunks of wood landed around us. My ears rang, and my head ached from the sheer intensity of the blast. Once it had settled, he jumped up, pulling me up and inspecting my body.

"Are you alright?" he asked with concern thick in his voice.

"I-I'm fine, what happened?" I resounded in a state of shock.

A cloud of dust was still floating throughout the field, making it look hazy. I could hear coughing as people attempted to breathe past the polluted air. We looked around the crowd, which was slowly standing. Those who had been at the back of the group had obvious signs of injuries. Several had blood pooling down their faces, while others stayed on the ground.

"Search the area! Find Sienna!" Forest commanded.

I looked to where Sienna had been. All that remained were the two guards holding their heads. I rushed down to them, Forest right behind me. I came to the first one and noticed the back of his head was bleeding. I wrapped my hand around his head, applying pressure.

"Where is Sienna?" Forest asked them in a severe tone.

"We're sorry, Alpha. When the explosion went off, I was hit in the head. It stunned me enough that she was able to slip away."

"Who would have hit them?" I asked, concerned.

Forest looked around the crowd. "Find me, Cliff, and Opal Ridge, now!"

Her parents? Would they have done that? Of course, they would; it was their daughter's life at stake. But at what cost? Would they make a run for it? Questions raced through my mind as I observed the chaos around us. Luckily, wolves recover quickly, and after some minor first aid on the spot, most of those present were well enough to head home. A few who had been close to the blast needed to go to the clinic for more severe injuries where the splinters of wood had embedded in their bodies. After I saw the last of the injured off, I walked over to Forest, who was standing with a group of warriors.

"It appears to have been some type of rudimentary explosive

device strapped to the back of the tree over there," Oakley informed him. "It may take a few days to collect all of the evidence as there is a wide spread of debris."

"I want everyone on this," Forest replied. "Call in all of the warriors. I want a team working on the explosion site, a team questioning each person in this pack, and the rest hunting down Sienna and her parents. I want them found now!"

I had never heard such anger in his voice before, but I understood where it was coming from, especially if he could not be sure that no one else had taken part. I stepped up to him and rubbed his back with my hand. I could feel his tense muscles loosen slightly under my touch. Once everyone had left to do their assigned jobs, he turned to look at me. His hard exterior softened somewhat, giving way to the concern I felt through the bond.

"I can't believe they did this," he said solemnly. "I never saw it coming."

"You couldn't have. You trust your pack. No one expects to be betrayed by those you're closest to. We're just lucky no one was killed."

He held his chin with his large hand and rubbed it, looking back at the jagged tree stump, all that was left from the explosion. I could feel the emotional turmoil inside of him. A mixture of anger, sadness, and determination swirled in my gut from him. He would not give up until he brought them back.

"What will you do to them when you find them?" I questioned.

"There is only one punishment for a betrayal such as this."

I didn't need him to tell me. I already knew. He would kill them —all of them. I could help them find them; I was a witch, after all. We had tracking spells that could tell us which direction they had gone, the same one I had been worried about my coven using on me. But I battled with my own morals, bringing them to their deaths. Could I do it?

"I..." I trailed off, still battling.

Perhaps if I were honest with him, he would understand my predicament. I was sure he could feel my turmoil inside of him as I felt his. He looked at me, brows scrunched together.

"What is it?" He asked worriedly.

I rubbed my cheek with my hand.

"I can find them for you if you need, but...I'm not sure I'm comfortable doing it only for them to be killed. My coven and I are peaceful people. We promote the balance of life. It...it's just hard for me to think that I could help bring someone to their death."

I looked past my lashes at him, fearing he would be disappointed in me. But his softened features brought an ease back to me. He did not look angry, but quite the opposite.

"You don't need to do that. We can find them. I don't want you to do anything you're uncomfortable with."

I could feel my shoulders relax. I was so relieved to hear him say that. I knew honesty would be the best choice. He pulled me close and kissed the top of my head. We stayed like that for a minute, taking some time for ourselves before he pulled back.

"Why don't you go back up to the house? I will be out here for a while," he said, exhausted.

"I want to help however I can."

"There is not much else to do right now. I already have my guys cleaning up and collecting evidence. The rest are on patrol or looking for them. I'm going to go out and see if I can help track them down."

I could feel myself worrying for him, but I knew that this was something he had to do.

"Alright, I might stop at the clinic to see if Dr. Stone needs help."

He smiled at me, "That would be great. Thank you. I also want someone with you until we find them."

"Why?" I questioned.

"Sienna is upset and acting irrationally. I won't take any risks."

"Okay."

I wasn't thrilled at it, but I admitted that I would feel a little safer. She had so much hate in her eyes for me when I saw her, and as Forest pointed out, if she were willing to go to this extreme, it would be better not to be cornered by her if she came after me. I didn't think I could fight off a wolf.

"August," he called to a group of warriors examining the tree.

August jogged over to us.

"Yes, Alpha."

"I want you to stay with Juniper."

"Of course, Alpha."

He looked at me and lowered his head, "Luna."

I smiled back, thankful that he was willing to stick with me through this when there were more important tasks at hand. We stopped at the gardens so that I could collect some healing herbs before walking back to the main street, where we found the clinic. The waiting room had several people in it. A few had blood on their clothing, but I didn't see any visible injuries. Perhaps they had brought people in. I looked up at the counter and saw Aurora standing behind it. I walked up to her.

"Luna, how can we help you?"

She seemed surprised to see me.

"I wanted to see if the doctor needed any help."

A smile spread across her face. "That is so nice of you. I'm not sure how much you can help with. We have six people checked in right now. Only one is serious. I will check with him."

"I can help heal if needed."

She looked at me, and realization dawned on her face, "You can do that?"

"Well, little things. I can help with infections and cleansing the blood."

"That's wonderful. Let me check with the doctor and see what he says."

"Great, thank you."

She walked down the hallway as I waited at the counter. A minute later, she returned, waving me down the hallway.

"This way, Luna."

August trailed behind me down the hall, and we entered a room towards the back. We walked into a small locker room. She handed me a set of scrubs and another set to August.

"If you two can change into these, please do. Dr. Stone is in surgery right now, and it is a sterile environment. I will wait outside for you."

"Thank you," I said, taking the scrubs.

"I will wait outside until you're dressed," August said, taking his scrubs.

I quickly dressed and swapped with August. Once we were both properly dressed in our scrubs, Aurora led us to a room with sinks and cabinets. There was a large window looking into the next room. Dr. Stone stood beside a table with an unconscious man lying on it. Another nurse stood opposite him. Aurora pushed a button on the wall near the door and spoke into it.

"Dr. Stone, I have the Luna here for you."

He looked over at the window. "Luna, thank you for coming in. Aurora said you could help with the infection?"

I quickly collected myself from the shock of the scene before me.

"Yes, although I'm unsure I can do it in a sterile environment. I have some herbs that I will need to use. Would that be allowed?"

"Did you bring them in with you?"

"I did. They're in my pocket."

"Perhaps we can do it after we bring him out of surgery," he thought aloud.

"I have several patients checked in. They had wood fragments embedded in their bodies. Their immune systems should take care of it, but if you can treat them for any infections, that would be best."

"Of course."

"Aurora, show her to the rooms. Assist her if she needs it."

"Yes, doctor."

She led us back down the hallway and into the first room, which was nearly identical to the one I had stayed in. A teenage girl lay on the bed and looked up at us when we walked in. Both of her arms were wrapped in gauze and resting on top of a blanket.

"Hello, Sky, the Luna has come to help you."

"Luna!" she said, surprised, and lowered her head. "Thank you for your help."

I smiled at her. "Your name is Sky? That's beautiful."

She smiled back at me, "Thank you."

I pulled up a chair near her bed and took a seat.

"I can help make sure that you don't get any infections. It would mean that I use a spell on you. Are you alright with that?"

Her jaw dropped. "Uh, yeah...will it hurt?"

"No. I will just rub some herbs on your forehead and speak some words."

"Okay."

I looked back at Aurora. "Would her parents be alright if I did this? I don't want to cross any boundaries."

"I live with my aunt. She is here too," Sky interjected.

"Is there any way we can ask her?"

"I will go ask," Aurora replied and turned out the door.

I looked back at Sky. "How are you doing? Is there any pain?"

"I'm alright. It hurts a little," her face turned more somber. "It was so sudden. One minute, we were standing there, and then the next, I was on the ground. It hurt so bad at first."

I gently took her hand, rubbing it with my thumb.

"It was a terrible thing that happened, and I am sorry you were hurt."

"Why did it happen?" she asked sadly.

"They are looking into it, but I think sometimes desperate people make bad decisions."

She looked down at the blanket and pursed her lips. I could see her eyes begin to water.

"What is important is that everyone is safe now," I added.

She looked back up at me and forced a small smile. Aurora came in a minute later.

"Her aunt said it was all right."

"Thank you for checking," I told her before looking back at Sky. "Shall we begin?"

She nodded her head, and I stood up. I pulled some of the herbs out of my pocket and crushed them in my fingers over and over until I felt them turn mushy. I used my thumb and rubbed the pulp across her forehead, then closed my eyes and took a deep breath in before waving my hands over her body.

"*Glan an corp, cuir às dha olc. Chan eil ach fuil fhìor-ghlan air fhàgail. Le sin de na tocsainnean bidh e a' sruthadh gu sgiobalta gus am bi iad fallain a-rithist.*" I chanted over her.

"That's it," I said.

"That was crazy!" She exclaimed. "My whole body felt tingly."

"It does that," I smiled back at her.

"Thank you."

"I'm happy to help," I said before looking at Aurora. "Do you have a damp cloth for her to clean her forehead?"

She was standing there watching us with a stunned expression. She nodded her head for a split second.

"Y-yes, Luna."

She opened a drawer and found a washcloth, which she dampened in the nearby sink. She walked over to Sky and helped her wipe off the remnants of the herbs. She still looked down at Sky, trying to figure out what had just happened.

"Shall we move on to the next room?" I asked her.

"Uh, yes."

I held back a laugh at her reaction. We continued helping each of the other patients. By the time we reached the last one, Dr. Stone was wheeling the man who had been in surgery into another patient room.

"Can I help?" I asked, following him in.

"Mr. Burr was the worst of the injured. He had several fragments hit organs. We were able to clean out the wounds, remove all of the debris, and stitch them up. His accelerated healing should help, but his injuries are severe. Is there anything else you can do for him?" he asked me, looking concerned.

"Is it that serious?"

"Unfortunately, yes. I'm not sure he will survive the night. It will be touch and go from here."

I thought back to my teachings. My Gran had told me of an old spell where we could harness the power from the moon and push it into a person. If the person is a child of the moon, such as a witch or, I assume, a shifter, it gives them a spark of life force. It was draining on us, often making the one who performs the spell sleep for a day or two afterward, since we are a conduit for the energy, but that would not be a big deal.

"I can do something, but we will need to get him under the moonlight."

Everyone turned and looked at me, surprised.

"What will you do?" Dr. Stone questioned excitedly.

"I need to give him some of the moon's power."

Dr. Stone looked out the window. "The sun is setting now. We can move him back once it's dark."

"Okay. We will need a bowl of water, and do you happen to have a moonstone?"

"I can get the water, but I don't have a moonstone, not here. Perhaps Aspen has some in her store."

"I will go see."

August and I left them and walked across Main Street to Aspen's shop. It was closed, as were most of the stores.

I looked back at August. "Do you know where she is?"

"Let me link her."

His eyes seemed to glaze over momentarily before returning to normal.

"She says she has some. She will bring them to the clinic."

"Great!" I said, relieved.

We waited out front for her. She jogged up and handed me a beautiful rose gold necklace with a round moonstone hanging from it.

"Is this what you were looking for?" she asked.

"Yes, thank you, Aspen."

I could tell she was wondering what the rush was for a necklace at the clinic, but I didn't want to make a spectacle about it, so I kept the explanation to myself. We walked back into the clinic and made our way to Mr. Burr's room. Dr. Stone was checking on his vitals with a troubled look.

"He does not seem to be improving," he told us.

"The moon has risen. We can take him now," I said.

Aurora grabbed his IV bag while Dr. Stone pushed the bed back into the hallway and toward the back of the building. The door was too narrow for the bed to fit through, so August carefully lifted him in his arms and brought him outside. I grabbed his blanket off the bed and laid it on the ground.

"Set him here," I said.

The others stepped back as I kneeled, placing the water bowl above his head and the moonstone on his chest.

I looked back at August, "I will probably sleep for a day or two after this. Just make sure Forest doesn't worry."

"Wait," he began to protest.

"Do not disturb me until it's done," I cut him off in a serious tone.

I rested one hand over the moonstone and lifted the other to the moon. I took a long, deep breath, blowing it out over Mr. Burr.

"*Selene, mo mhàthair. Thoir dhomh do sholas gus an urrainn dhomh beatha a thoirt air ais don leanabh agad. Cleachd mi mar do làmhan, do shùilean agus do bhodhaig. Thoir do thiodhlacan don leanabh agad. Is leatsa mo chorp-sa airson a chleachdadh airson do ghnìomh,*" I chanted.

I felt the first spark of the energy move through my body, traveling from one hand to the other. As I repeated the chant again, my whole body began to feel limp. The third time I chanted, I could tell that Selene had arrived. By the fourth chant, it felt as if I was watching from outside my body, and after the fifth and final chant, my body went slack, dropping to the ground. My mind returned to my body only to find darkness.

25

Forest

S ienna and her parents had been clever. After they ran from
the training field, they took to the forest, making a b-line to
the edge of our territory. They had made it to one of the
surrounding lakes and must have swam for it. We had been
circling the lake for any sign of where they would have climbed
out. I was tracking the single trail that had come in this direction
with a small group, telling me that they split up. I knew the smell
as Opal. She should be easy enough to find. The sun was beginning to set, making the surrounding forest dark, but it did not
hinder our search. Our enhanced eyesight and impeccable sense
of smell made it easy to follow her.

*Alpha, we have accounted for all of the pack members and have
come up with one shorter than expected,* Oakley linked me.

I stopped in my tracks.

Who is it?

Flint Haywood.

Flint Haywood was the high school science teacher. Why would he be missing?

Check his house.

We already did. I need to tell you that it seems that he built the explosive. We found the materials in his basement.

My wolf growled. Why would he do something like this? Then it dawned on me.

He's her mate, I linked back to Oakley.

Whose?

Sienna's. He has to be her mate. It's the only explanation for him committing his crimes. No one would give up their entire life and pack unless it was for their mate. Check the Ridge's house and see if you can pick up his scent there. They obviously were in on it together.

Yes, Alpha.

Listen up, I linked to the search party. *We are looking for four people: Sienna, her parents, and Flint Haywood.*

We continued on our search. I knew those still searching the lake would now be looking for Haywood along with the others. Opal's scent was getting stronger, meaning she had been here recently. I pushed harder, determined to find her. Up ahead, I could make out the sound of a small wolf weaving through the trees. We had her.

Don't take her yet. Let her lead us to the others, I told the rest of my group.

We slowed just enough so we could continue following without alerting her to our presence. The sun had fully set, and the moon had begun to rise when I felt my body start to tingle. It became so strong that it took my breath away. What could possibly be causing this? I slowed, not wanting to misstep and alert Opal to our presence. The others slowed with me.

Go ahead of me. Don't lose her, I told them.

I stopped and attempted to regain myself, shaking my head as if I could chase the feeling away. Nothing helped. Suddenly, it felt like every drop of my energy drained from my body. Even a single step seemed like a chore. I needed to get a grip on whatever was happening to me and fast. I sat down, giving myself a moment to recover. Something was wrong, and if I did nothing to bring this on, what was it? Juniper...

Juniper, where are you at? I tried to link her.

Nothing...

Juniper, answer me, please.

Warning bells started to go off in my head.

August, where is Juniper? I demanded.

She is here at the clinic.

Still? She should have been long done with whatever she could help with.

What happened to her?

She did some type of spell. We were about to lose Callan Burr. She said that she may be asleep for a day or two afterward.

And you didn't think to stop her? I screamed through the link.

I apologize, Alpha.

Is she okay?

She is resting. Dr. Stone examined her and said that everything seemed fine. Would you like me to take her back to the house?

No! I'm on my way. Make sure Dr. Stone closely monitors her until I get there.

Yes, Alpha.

I was furious. How could they let her do something so reckless? She would have been feeling what I was, but much more intensely. No wonder she was unconscious. I was uncertain whether I had enough energy to get back. The only thing giving me the motivation to keep going was my need to get to her. Adrenaline coursed through my body like an addictive fuel. Even if I had all my energy, it would take me at least an hour to return. I could only think about everyone's consequences for allowing her to take such a risk.

By the time I made it to town, my anger had built so strongly that I knew I would rip the head off of anyone in my way. My fellow pack members would be able to sense how angry their Alpha was and would be sure to give me a wide berth. I jogged through town, pushing open the clinic doors with my head. Once inside, I shifted back to my human form.

"Find me some clothes, now!" I snapped at Aurora, who was standing behind the counter.

"Yes, Alpha," she quickly replied before running down the same hallway I was walking down.

I could feel the bond pull me to one of the rooms to the right, and I opened the door. August was standing beside it on the inside, and Dr. Stone was next to the bed; both held their heads down, being sure not to make eye contact. They both could feel the anger pouring off of me. Just then, Aurora came in with a set of scrubs. I threw them on and approached Juniper, who was resting peacefully in the bed. I ran my hand down her face, feeling the familiar sparks travel up my arm, calming me slightly. I turned back and glared at the others.

"Why the hell would you let her do something so dangerous?"

"I apologize, Alpha," Dr. Stone stepped forward. "We did not realize it would drastically affect her until she was already beginning."

"Why did you not stop her then?" I asked, not satisfied with his explanation.

"I started to," August added, "but she stopped me. She demanded that she not be interrupted. I feared that something could happen to her if I did. She had told me not to let you worry."

I let out a deep sigh. I was still extremely angry and frustrated, but I could not argue at the moment. If they thought stopping what she did would have been a larger risk to her, then they did the right thing, whether I liked it or not.

"Is she able to go home?" I asked Dr. Stone.

"Yes, Alpha. She is simply in a deep sleep."

I carefully picked her up in my arms and walked out the door, not saying another word to anyone as we exited. I saw several people out and about who stopped to look at us, but I gave them no second thought. I'm sure they were worried after all of today's events, but all I had left in me was to take care of my mate. Halfway to the pack house, one of my men mind-linked me.

Alpha, we have apprehended both Cliff and Opal Ridge.

What about Sienna and Flint Haywood?

There is no sign of them yet.

Where did you find them?

They met at an old trapper's cabin. We planned on waiting to see if the others showed up, but the wind changed, and Opal and Cliff caught our scent. They attempted to run, but we captured them. We are bringing them in.

Keep some scouts around the cabin and have them report in immediately if Sienna or Flint shows up.

Yes, Alpha.

I adjusted Juniper to open the front door and took her straight to the apartment. She was wearing the same light blue scrubs that I was. I carefully changed her into her pajamas and tucked her into bed. My blood was racing through me too quickly for me to calm down, but I still pulled myself into the bed next to her. The entire day had been one problem after another. Holding onto Juniper eventually calmed me enough to go through today's events adequately. Cliff and Opal Ridge begging me for leniency, Juniper's grandmother looking for her...

Shit! I had forgotten about her. I never even told Juniper about her showing up. If she sleeps for a day or two, she may miss the chance to see her. I can only hope she wakes in time. If not, perhaps I can ask her grandmother to wait a few more days, but how can I do that without making her suspicious? I don't want her to think we are keeping her here or using her for her magic.

Would she accept that Juniper used her magic on us? This was a whole new complication tacked on to my day. One that I could not solve until tomorrow, though. For now, all I wanted and needed was to hold my mate.

WITHOUT HER STEADY breathing throughout the night, I would have worried more about Juniper. She had not moved once since I brought her back. It was as if she were in some type of coma, completely disconnected from the world. I stayed next to her, watching her for the first part of the morning. I knew that I needed to get up and attend to my responsibilities, but I could not bring myself to be away from her while she was like this. She was vulnerable, and the danger of having Sienna out there dug into my natural instinct to protect her.

Are there any signs of Sienna or Flint? I linked Oakley, who had been in charge of the situation throughout the night.

It was times like these that he truly showed his worth. He was an excellent Beta, and while his humor often got him in trouble, I knew I could rely on him without a second thought.

We found their trails from the lake. They merged about two miles on the far side of it. They seem to be keeping to the water because we lost their trail again at the next lake. We've been out here all night, but have been unable to detect where they went. I think they may have stuck to the streams.

Dammit!

Okay, I'll send a new group to take over. You guys can get back to eating and resting.

Yes, Alpha.

I should be out there helping... Before Juniper, nothing would have kept me from leading the search party. What if something happened to them while I was back here? I growled in frustration and punched the nearby door. My fist went straight through it, sending ruminants flying into the hallway. I snapped my eyes towards Juniper, not even a flinch. I ran my hand down my face. I felt like I was losing it. On one hand, I had my mate to protect; on the other, I had my pack to lead. I needed to figure out how to do both. If the most significant danger was Sienna, I needed to find her and end the threat. I couldn't do that from my bedroom.

August, I want you and three other warriors posted at my apartment to protect Juniper. I'm heading out with the next search party.

Yes, Alpha.

This was the only thing I could come up with. Hopefully, it was the right choice. Once August and the others arrived, I gave them strict instructions to let me know as soon as she woke before I took off with the others. They had gone to the eastern lakes, around forty kilometers, as the bird flew over steep mountain terrain. We found them relatively easy. They gave us the rundown of their search so far so that we could pick up where they left off. We would be heading north up the river. I had a group on either side checking for any signs of the fugitives.

The river was fairly shallow, with rocky shores on either side. Tall mountains full of thick forest flanked it as far as could be seen. We fanned out on either side to cover the forest, the shores, and the water. Because of how shallow it was, it would be easy enough for them to run straight up it. We would need to find the exact point at which they moved away from the water. It was our only chance.

After half the day had passed, we traveled another forty kilometers upriver. At this point, it would take me at least two to three hours to get home. I needed to handle the situation with Juniper's grandmother before it got too late. I instructed the others to keep at it until nightfall and then head back the way we came to give it a second go-over. If we hadn't found them by then, there was a good chance they had gotten away from us, at least for now. I turned heel and ran towards the nearby col, heading back home. I had just about peaked it when August linked me.

Alpha, the Luna is starting to wake.

Thank the Goddess!

That's good. Get the doctor there to check on her. I'll be back as soon as I can.

Yes, Alpha.

I pushed harder, wanting to be there for her and ask her what the hell she had been thinking.

26

Juniper

My eyes felt heavy as my mind began to awake. I tried to open them but struggled, letting out a small sigh instead. I could faintly hear a door open. I heard someone speak as if through a thick blanket, making it sound muffled. I could not tell what they were saying, nor could I respond yet. It felt like my body was trying to reboot. I let out a long breath and focused on my fingers. I attempted to move them, finding it difficult. I could only make out the slightest twitch rather than lifting them. Another sigh escaped my lips. I tried again and again. Slowly, it felt as if they were waking up. I could lift my index finger maybe an inch before it fell back to the bed. With more attempts, I felt my middle finger begin to move. Soon, I could lift each finger for a split second. Even these tiny movements felt exhausting. I decided to give myself a break, trying to find the energy to continue.

Suddenly, I could hear a commotion coming from a distance.

Someone was yelling, but I couldn't make out who it was. Were they trying to talk to me? No...It seemed that there were at least two voices, maybe more, yelling. After several thuds, it went completely silent. I focused on my hearing to try and see what was happening around me. Another voice suddenly sounded very close, as if it were right beside me. I felt a harsh sting on my cheek. I wanted to reach up and hold it but still couldn't move my body. It sounded like someone was yelling at me, but again, I could not make it out. I felt something move under me. I realized someone was lifting me. Was it Forest? It didn't feel like him. Whosever arms these were were much smaller, and I felt no sparks. I felt us moving quickly.

"Hey, put her down!" I could make out the words, though they were still muffled.

What was happening? I used everything I had to open my eyes. There was a man that I did not recognize holding me. I wanted to scream, to fight, but my eyes fell closed again. Another thud. What just happened? Who had yelled? It didn't sound like Forest, but it seemed familiar. I tried to move my body again, but it had no effect. I began to feel drained. I could feel my mind slipping. Not yet! I needed to do something. To stop whoever it was. I tried to take a deep breath and chant an incantation in my thoughts.

Stad an corp, air a chumail sàmhach. Cuir stad orra bho bhith a' gluasad gus an tèid innse dhaibh, I thought in my mind.

There was a slight falter in the man's step, but he continued. How could I expect to cast a spell if I didn't have the energy to move or even open my eyes? It required energy and focus. I needed to be centered, which, in my current condition, would not be easy to accomplish. In my attempt to freeze the person who had taken me, I used the little energy I had been building, and all went silent as I slipped back into the darkness.

~

Forest

I HAD MADE it a few steps down the backside of the col when I felt a sting on my cheek. Strange...I thought to myself. There were no branches or twigs to whip at my face, and Juniper was just waking up. There would be no reason for the sensation I had felt to have come from her. I gave it no further thought as I traversed down the rocky incline, being careful where I stepped so as not to cause a rock slide. As I neared the bottom, I felt someone trying to mind-link me. It was like a spark of a connection, but no one said anything. I wondered if it had been Juniper trying to wake up.

Juniper? I called through the connection.

A-alph...

I could barely make it out. I stopped and focused on it. I could feel each of my pack members through the link. I felt for Juniper. I could feel her, but she was not trying to contact me. I focused on August next, as he was the one guarding her. I could feel the connection wanting to be made, but seemingly unable to.

August? I called to him.

A-Alpha.

He sounded weak, injured...

What's wrong? I immediately asked, worry burning through me.

If something had happened to him, then that would mean...

August, talk to me. Where is Juniper?

T-taken...

Fuck!

Oakley! I called through my mind.

Alpha, he responded.

I could tell from his groggy response that I must have woken him.

Get to my apartment now! Something's happened.

Yes, Alpha, he responded more alert this time.

I began racing as fast as I could, calling back to the group I had left to return to the pack. I could stick to the valleys the rest of the way, allowing my wolf to move at nearly full speed, but it would still take me at least another forty-five minutes. Too long to rescue Juniper if something had happened to her.

Alpha, there's been an attack, Oakley reported. *All of the guards and August are down. There is a slight smell of something in the air. I think a gas was used.*

And Juniper? I asked, already knowing the answer.

She's gone...

My heart felt like it cracked in two. I had failed her. My job as her mate was to protect her. I would give up everything for her. I could not imagine my life without her. I howled to the darkening sky as I ran. I could hear the faint call of my pack in the distance, responding to my grief.

Find her! I commanded Oakley.

On it, Alpha.

My breathing was turning jagged as my wolf panicked, and I pushed my body to its limits. I could feel myself begin to lose control of the beast inside me. Beyond my emotional battle, I was now struggling with my wolf, who wanted to find his mate by any means necessary. I could not allow that. He would kill anyone who crossed his path, including our pack members. I tried to push reason into him. The wolf inside me was more animal, responding to emotions the strongest. I had reeled him just enough when I neared our town.

Alpha, we followed their trail to the service road over the mountain. They got in a car and headed towards the city.

I growled. There was no way for us to track them by car. They were gone. What can I do? How can I find her? I met the others at the pack house. Almost every warrior had gathered out front, waiting for my orders. They cleared a path for me as I shifted, stormed up the drive, and threw the door open. I could hear it crack and splinter from the force. Oakley and August were waiting inside the foyer for me.

"What do we have?" I wasted no time asking them.

"We can tell they headed south towards the city. I have five cars out on the roads looking for them, but we don't know what type of car we are looking for. The ground was too dry to get a good take on the tire impressions." Oakley reported.

I looked over at August, who had his head lowered.

"What happened?" I asked him, feeling a surge of anger.

"I failed you, Alpha. Some type of canister was tossed into the apartment. We rushed to open the windows, but it was too power-ful. Each of us passed out before we could clear the gas."

My fists clenched at my sides. How the hell did they get gas canisters? His head lowered further as another growl escaped my lips. For how angry I was at him for allowing something to happen to her, the logical part of my brain realized that he was up against forces beyond nature. Sienna and Flint were playing dirty, using chemical warfare against us, a taboo in wolf culture. It was the only way that they could have gotten past our forces.

"How did they get back on territory?" I asked.

"They must have known the patrol schedule in order to slip by. We found their scent on the west side."

Sienna probably knew too much about how our pack ran from all her time with me and at the pack house. For all I knew, she had gone through my files. This was all my fucking fault. I ran my hand down my face, fighting the frustration I felt.

"I want everyone on this. Get someone on every computer Flint had access to. He had to research this stuff. I wanted to know what else he had been looking at. The same goes for Cliff and Opal. I want double patrols until this gets sorted. We need to set up a new schedule, one unfamiliar to them. Anyone else still available should be searching the surrounding area for any sign of them."

"Yes, Alpha," they both responded and darted out the front door.

I would find her. Nothing would get in my way...

27

Juniper

A fresh wave of energy flowed through me as I woke again. I flittered my eyes open. It was dark. I could just make out the slight details of a darkened, unfamiliar room. The only source of illumination was the dance of moonlight streaming in through a window. That at least explained my renewed energy. I tried to reach my arm forward to touch it but found that it was bound behind my back. I struggled against my restraints.

"Look who's finally woken up!" a high-pitched, sinister voice echoed off the bare wooden walls.

I peered in the direction it came from and gasped at the glowing golden eyes. A swipe of a match flicked a dim light into the room. Whoever held it moved it into a lantern sitting on an old, rickety table in the middle of the room. Once lit, the flame grew, allowing my eyes to take in the tall blonde standing behind it. Sienna...

"Where am I?" I croaked out.

My voice was horse and dry.

"Nowhere anyone can find you," she said, gloating.

"Why did you take me?"

"What's with all the questions? I'm not here for that."

"Then what are you here for?"

"If you have to ask that, you're dumber than I thought."

"I understand you're mad about me mating with Forest, but don't you think this is taking things too far?" I asked as I pulled myself up, leaning against the rough wall.

I realized my ankles were also tied together. The realization of my situation was sobering, fully waking me up.

"You didn't just take away Forest from me. You took my position in the pack! If it weren't for you, I would have become Luna!"

"Forest told me things were never serious with you."

"That's bullshit. The bed we pulled you from...yeah, we fucked in there every single night for years before you showed up. That was my bed."

A quick memory resurfaced: black lace...It all started clicking into place. Sienna's bra, the pain I felt when I assumed that I was the other woman. My stomach twisted, but then I recalled Forest's explanation. She did not live there. Sure, she stayed over, but he had never given her the right to live there, to bring in her stuff. I trusted Forest and knew she only spouted more lies to torment me.

"No, that's not what he said," I shot back at her confidently.

"Of course, it's not. What would he tell the person he thought was his new mate? 'Oh, by the way, I've spent the last two and a half years with Sienna, fucking her in every nook and cranny of the pack house. But don't mind it.' You're such a stupid whore. Bewitching him in one of your spells, trying to make him your own. Well, I'll tell you what. You messed with the wrong she-wolf. I will make you pay for ever looking in his direction and screwing my whole life up!"

"I swear I didn't bewitch him or cast any spell. It just happened," I argued back.

"That's enough!" She screamed at me. "As soon as I kill you, your whole charade will be over, and he will take me back with open arms, happy that I rid him of your curse."

My breath hitched at her threat. Was she really going to kill me? I needed to stop her. I took a deep breath and began to chant.

"*Stad an corp, air a chumail sàmhach. Cuir stad.*"

Smack!

My whole face felt like it was on fire. I could taste a hint of copper in the back of my mouth and a trickle down my lips. I opened my eyes to see her standing over me.

"Don't think you can cast one of your spells on me, witch."

She walked across the room, grabbing a strip of rope off a far counter. "We'd better make sure you don't try that again."

"No, stop," I pleaded before she grabbed my hair, slamming my head against the wall.

My world spun from the impact. I could feel the rough rope tug at the corner of my mouth as she fastened it tightly around my head. I tried to talk, but it came out a blubbering mess of words, the clarity long gone. Would my incantations still work?

I tried again, "*Sa a cope.*"

Another brutal hit to the face. I bit down on the rope, fighting back the tears that threatened to fall. The pain in my face was excruciating. I leaned back against the wall, trying to find some relief, but to no avail. There was nothing I could do. I was at her mercy. Sienna walked around the room, laughing at my pain.

"Poor little witch. This is what you get for screwing with someone else's life. Don't worry. You won't last much longer. The only reason we didn't kill you on the spot is that I wanted Forest to worry a little. I mean, after all, he did condemn me to my death. I want him to know the type of pain I felt when he chose you over me. But count your minutes because these will be your last."

The tears won. I felt the first fall down my cheek.

"Oh, look at you, cry," she said condescendingly, "Don't worry, I'm only going to give him a day or so before I finish you off."

She looked at her nails as if this was nothing more than an annoyance. My breathing increased.

Forest, I called out to him.

Nothing came back. I felt a sob escape my bound lips. Why wasn't he answering me?

"Agh, I'm so tired of your dramatics! They don't work on me. You're nothing more than a slut, a whore, who weaseled her way into the wrong pack."

She walked to the door that was half off its hinges and looked back at me.

"Now, don't try and escape. I don't think you stand a chance against a wolf," she snarled at me.

She walked out, leaving me to dwell on my fate. I finally allowed myself to let go of all of the emotions I had held inside. I let out a loud cry, dropping my head down towards the ground. Everything felt hopeless. I could do nothing to save myself. Tears poured down my face. I thought back to Forest. His warm, inviting dark brown eyes lured me into his soul, his thick mane of black hair that I loved to run my fingers through, and his soft lips caressing my own. The thought of him made me cry harder.

Forest, please....

Still nothing. Why would he not answer me? Was something wrong? Was he hurt? There is no way he would have let them take me, was there?

Finally, after a long while, I gathered enough courage and confidence to try loosening the bindings around my ankles. They were so tight I couldn't even move. I managed to stand up, but could only take small hops around the room. There was no way I could escape into the forest like this. I started scanning the room for a tool I could use. There were old wooden boards for the walls and floor. A stone fireplace sat in the center of the far wall, and the only furniture was the table, a couple of chairs I wouldn't trust sitting in, and a small bed frame in the corner. Several cabinets lined one wall. Maybe they had what I needed. I hopped across the room, nearly falling over once or twice. I turned my back to the cabinets so I could grab the handles. I tugged at the first one, but it wouldn't budge. I pulled harder. It finally swung open, pulling out of its space and sending me along with its contents, falling to the ground. A heavy drawer hit my spine, causing a sharp pain to shoot up my back. I groaned as I rolled onto my side. I slowly sat up, fighting through the pain in my back.

I looked on the floor, finding an old wooden spoon and nothing else. I pursed my lips against the rope and let out a sigh. All of that for a spoon. I worked my way back up and tried the next drawer. Luckily, this one quickly opened and displayed the box of matches Sienna must have used. I leaned backward over the drawer to pick up the box and sat on the floor. I held it in my left hand and pushed with my right, sliding it open. I felt proud of myself for my accomplishment. I carefully pulled a match out and tried to strike it against the side of the box. Having my hands bound made this exceptionally difficult. After nervous matches and tries, I hear the spark come to life. I maneuvered it to my wrists, trying to burn the rope. I could feel the flame flicker on my skin, and a burning sensation grew around my wrists. I adjusted the match but realized that I would have to deal with the pain to get through the rope. The smell of burning hair and flesh began to fill the room as it nipped at my hands and wrists. When the flame hit my fingertips, I dropped it, searching for the box of matches again.

I slid another match out and struck it quicker than the last. I brought it back to the rope at my wrist and held in a whimper from feeling the heat on what I believed was burned skin. The smell of burning chemicals from the rope mixed with the scent of

my skin carried through the air. I could feel a more intense sensation as I suspected the nylon fibers of the rope melted onto my
wrists. The flame touched my fingertips again, and I dropped it
once more. After several tries, I finally managed to pull the ropes
apart. I looked at the scorched and burnt flesh with nylon still
stuck to it. Even with a spell, it would take a while to heal. First, I
removed the rope from my mouth and then tried to untie the
ropes at my ankles, but again, they were tied too tightly. I grabbed
the box of matches and carefully burned my bindings away.

Once free, I peeked out the door, looking for any sign of
Sienna. I slowly crept out and hid behind the first bush I found. I
waited for a moment to see if she came looking for me. When
there was no sign, I pushed forward. I tried to move silently
through the overgrowth surrounding the dilapidated wood cabin I
had been in. I saw no other signs of life, so I could only guess
which way to go. All I knew was that I needed to get out of there. I
could find my way in the morning. I barely made it fifty feet when
a robust set of hands grabbed me from behind.

"Where do you think you're going?" a deep voice spoke.

"Let me go!" I screamed.

"Quiet!" He whispered in my ear. "If she hears you, she will kill
you right now."

I caught my breath. I wanted to yell, scream, and fight him off.
But I needed to know who this was. Was it one of the warriors?
Was he here to save me? I looked back at him. He was far smaller
than Forest but still fit. Where Forest had more of a thick build
with his impressive, large muscles, this man had a swimmer's
body, lean but defined. His eyes glared at me in warning.

"Who are you?" I whispered back at him.

"It doesn't matter," he said deadpan.

"A-are you here to save me?"

He didn't reply, but turned me around and led me back

towards the cabin. Realizing he was taking me back, I dug in my heels.

"Stop, you can't take me back!" I objected.

"I told you to be quiet," he said more angrily.

A newfound strength bubbled inside me, and I flung my head back, connecting with his chin. His grip loosened, and I took advantage and ran in the opposite direction. I pushed myself harder than ever, moving at what felt like super speed. The bushes and trees whipped at my face, tearing at my cotton pajamas. My bare feet screamed in protest as I felt sticks and thorns underneath them, but this was now life or death. I had to push forward.

Forest! I screamed to him through my mind.

Even without a reply, I continued running. I could hear the man behind me gaining on me. I darted to the right, then left, hoping that he would have a more challenging time catching me if I didn't travel in a straight line. Thinking it may be working, I let a little hope enter my heart when a shadow darted from the side, colliding with my body and sending me flying to the ground. The impact was hard and debilitating. I rolled onto my back and looked at the blonde wolf towering over me. I heard the crack of a bone, followed by another. Soon, it was Sienna standing completely nude over me.

"What did I tell you about running, you stupid little whore?"

She kicked my ribs hard, and I lost my breath from the impact. I swear I heard my rib crack. I grabbed it and rolled onto my side. She kicked me again and again. Everything went black when her foot collided with the side of my head.

28

Forest

We could not pick up on their trail after searching the road the car had traveled down. I was frustrated and felt hopeless that there was nothing more to do at that moment but run through the vast Canadian landscape looking for her. After two hours. I tried to link her over and over but could not reach her. She had to be either unconscious or too far away to mind link her. We could only use the link within fifty kilometers of each other. Usually, it would not be a problem as we did not often go beyond that. When we did, we either had wolves stationed at intervals to relay the message or used phones when we could. With the mate bond, I was still able to feel her, though, which made me think that she was still unconscious.

We regrouped at the pack house, brainstorming our next move. Maps were sprawled out on the main dining table, with all of my strongest warriors and trackers shouting their two cents. I sat silently, taking it all in and fighting the building rage inside me.

It was not their fault we hadn't found her yet. It was no one's fault but Sienna and Flint, both of whom I would be sure to punish in the worst possible way when I found them. I leaned forward, resting my forehead on my fist, my elbow propped up on the table.

"We need to make a decision," I said with a bite in my voice.

The room was silenced, and all eyes landed on me.

"We have no idea where they have gone. All we know is that there was no sign of them leaving the service road before it hit the main road. From there, it's..." Oakley trailed off.

"I know. We need to decide if we go north to the wilderness or south to the city."

"Both will be like finding a needle in a haystack," my lead warrior, Atlas, added.

"Do you think I don't know that?" I growled at him.

Everyone lowered their heads.

I sat back in my chair, scratching my head. I was hit with a hard pain in the front of my face. I grabbed at it with my hand. It felt as if my nose had broken. I checked my hand, expecting blood, but none could be found. I felt my nose with my fingers, realizing nothing was there. Juniper...It was not my pain but hers. When we felt the pain come through the mate bond, it was muted, never as strong as the pain the other felt. If I had experienced it that intensely, I could only imagine how hard it was for Juniper.

"Is everything alright, Alpha?" Oakley asked cautiously.

I ignored him, and instead, I focused on her, trying to link her.

Juniper, can you hear me?

Nothing. I let out a deep growl, making everyone around me shrink back into themselves. They watched me with worry, fearful that I would lash out. I dug my hands into my knees, feeling myself tear my pants and cut into my skin. I took a few breaths, trying to regain my composure, when I felt an ache in the side of my mouth. I closed my eyes, focusing on what it could be. I needed to know what was happening to her. The pain was concentrated on the edges of my mouth. My bottom lip felt as if it were being pulled. The pain radiated around my cheeks and wrapped around my head. They must have gagged her with something. I could feel another growl surging forward, but I fought it back. That was until I felt another hit to the face. I jumped up from my chair and began pacing back and forth, hoping it would stop there. After several minutes of no new pain, I stopped and looked at the warriors across the room.

"We are finding her now! They are hurting her."

Their eyes widened with worry and anger. With no plan in place, I searched my mind for anything we could do. I started pacing again, racking my mind about anything and everything we could do. I stopped, staring off into space. Her grandmother... maybe she could help. Why had I taken so long to think about her? I let out another growl and looked back at the others.

"I want a plan when I get back."

"Where are you going?" Oakley asked.

"To find help."

I took off from the room, grabbing one of the bags of clothes we kept near the door. Once outside, I stripped down, discarding my clothes on the ground and shifting into my wolf. I grabbed the bag with my teeth and took off to the Harper cabin. As I ran, I felt my forelimbs begin to burn just above my paws. Realizing that it was another pain coming through the bond, I pushed harder, not wanting to give them another second to hurt her. The lights of the cabin came into view. At least I knew she was there. I slowed, sniffing the air and checking for signs of others. When the only scent I picked up was that of Juniper's grandmother, I shifted and grabbed the clothes out of the bag. I quickly dressed and walked up to the porch, knocking on the door.

The older woman opened the door slightly, peeking through the crack. When she saw me, she opened it fully and looked me over.

"Where is Juniper?" she asked.

There was confidence and strength in her voice, but I could smell the slight twinge of fear from her.

"I need your help. Someone has taken her."

Her eyes widened, and she stepped back, holding the door open for me. I followed her to the sofa in the room.

"Tell me what happened," she demanded.

I divulged everything that had happened, being brutally honest with her. I could see anger in her eyes, but I was unsure if it was directed at me or the situation. When I finally finished, we sat in an awkward silence for a moment while I waited for her to respond.

"You believe that you are truly mates?"

"I know we are."

"I believe Juniper put a blocking spell on herself after she left with you so that we could not find her. If what you said about Heather was true, then I understand why she did it, but it means that I cannot use it now to find her. However..." she continued, "if you are truly mates, perhaps I can use the energy from your bond. It is like a string caught in space that ties the two of you together."

Just as I was about to respond, I felt a hard hit on my side. All of the air in my lungs was forced out of it. Juniper's grandmother rushed over to me, touching my back. I felt a hard hit to my ribs, followed by another and another. It felt like it went on forever until, finally, it halted. I looked up at the woman with pleading eyes. She understood what I was trying to tell her.

"Please, ma'am, do whatever you must to find her. I don't know if she will last much longer."

"Call me Magnolia," she said before going to the counter.

She opened a bag sitting atop it and pulled out a jar of dried white flowers. She opened it again and pulled several out, returning them to me.

"Give me your hand," she demanded.

My wolf did not like being told what to do, but was as desperate as I was to find Juniper and let it go. She crushed the flower in my palm and closed my fingers around it.

"I am going to try and strengthen your bond. It should allow you to feel where she is at."

I nodded my head at her. She wrapped her hands around my closed fist that held the flowers. She closed her eyes and began to chant.

"*An ceangal a chruthaich thu, leig leis fàs mar shìol. Fosgail an uinneag bho aon inntinn gu inntinn eile. Leig leotha fhaicinn mar an tè eile, leig leotha faireachdainn a bhith a 'tighinn a-steach, gu bràth is barrachd,*" She repeated three times.

As the last word escaped her lips, I felt a power surge in my chest. A forceful breath was pulled into my lungs as if it were my first. My world felt like it had broadened, sensing things I had never felt before. I looked up at her with wide eyes.

"It appears to have worked," she smiled.

"What do I do now?"

"You need to focus on her. You should be able to feel her."

I closed my eyes and thought of Juniper. It was like a string tightened to my chest, pulling me north.

"I can feel her!"

"Then you must go save her."

I jumped up and raced to the door. I stopped and looked back at her.

"Can you wait here for her? I know she would want to see you."

"I will wait. Now go and save my granddaughter."

I nodded once and shifted as I jumped off the old wooden porch, shredding the clothes I had been wearing, and raced into the trees.

Everyone, head north! I will meet you near the main road, I linked to my warriors as I serpentined through the thick forest.

Juniper

I woke as the man set me back on the ground in the same rickety cabin I had escaped from. I groaned from the ache in my ribs. This whole being knocked unconscious deal needed to stop happening. In the last couple of weeks, I had found myself in the darkness of my own mind too many times.

"You have to be quiet. It was stupid of you to run," he grunted out.

"Who are you? Why are you helping her?" I asked desperately.

He looked down at the ground, almost as if he were ashamed.

"Please, why are you doing this to me?"

He looked back up at me with sadness in his eyes.

"I'm not like this...usually."

"Then why are you doing it now?" I asked a little more calmly.

Perhaps I could sway him into helping me.

"She's my mate..."

"Who? Sienna?"

"Yes. We found each other right after we turned eighteen. She told me she was not ready for our bond and avoided me afterward. It felt like my soul was crushed when she said those words to me, but I always held out hope that she would come around. She never rejected me."

"What about her and Forest?"

He gripped his hair at the memory.

"It was the most painful thing I had ever experienced. I felt it every time they were together."

I was shocked, "Why did you stay?"

"I thought about leaving every single day. But where would I go? I could ask for a transfer to another pack, but that would have required me to sit down with the Alpha. I couldn't bring myself to do it every time I tried."

I could hear the pain in his voice as he retold his story.

He began pacing the room and continued, "When you showed up, she came to me. I had thought she was finally coming back to me, and we could put everything behind us. She promised me that once we had gotten rid of you, we would run off to another pack and be together. She said that she could no longer live in a pack where she felt rejected by everyone."

"And you went along with it?"

"Not initially. I told her I couldn't hurt the Luna but was still there for her. She stormed off from me, and that's when you two had the run-in at the diner. After that, she was taken to the cells. Everyone knew that she would be put to death for threatening you. I was scared. Even though she put me through all that, I had thought that if I could save her, we could run away and finally be together. I couldn't let my mate die."

He continued, "I knew how to make small explosions. It only took a little extra research to find out how to make the bomb. I needed it as a distraction to get her out of there. One they wouldn't be expecting. The night before her sentencing, I hid it in the tree, covering its scent with mud. When you pardoned her, I felt like a weight was lifted off my chest. I thought she could do her time, and then we could start again."

"What about her whole speech about wanting to be the Luna? You can't possibly think she had changed her mind after that?" I chastised, though it was probably the wrong approach if I wanted to get him to help me.

His glare seemed to prove my thought correct.

"She's just confused. I-I know she will choose me!" he nearly screamed at me. "You're just like all the others. I know her. She's my mate. She was made to want me, to love me! Not the stupid

Alpha. He just used her. He tossed her aside as soon as something better came along. She will see he's worthless to her."

At the end of his rant, he rushed out of the cabin, leaving me alone. I looked around and realized that in his emotional haste, he had forgotten entirely to retie me. I felt my ribs, trying to gauge if I would be able to manage another attempt at escaping. They were sore but felt surprisingly better already.

Juniper, can you hear me? Forest's voice spoke in my head.

I cried out in relief and threw my hand over my mouth, not wanting Sienna or her mate to hear me.

Forest! I can hear you. Where are you?

I'm coming for you!

I could feel him. It felt like the same pull that initially brought me to him, but substantially stronger, almost as if I could feel what he was doing. I closed my eyes and focused on him. I could see the trees flying by him, his wolf's snout in front of him, and his paws thundering under him. I could hear others with him. They were moving quickly, and I could feel them getting closer.

I can see you. How is this possible?

Your grandmother.

What? I exclaimed.

How could she have helped? Was she here?

How?

She came to find you. I told her what happened, and she strengthened our bond so that I could find you.

Tears flowed from my eyes. My Gran was here. Forest was coming to save me. Hope coursed through me.

I can try to escape and meet you, I offered.

Where are they now?

I don't know. I think they are outside somewhere. I'm in an old cabin.

Stay there. You won't be able to outrun them. Can you barricade yourself in?

I looked around the room once more.

No. There is not enough furniture, and they would only push it in.

See if you can hide somewhere. We should be there soon.

Okay. Forest...

Yes?

I love you

I could feel my heart tighten and surge with warmth. I realized it was him.

I love you too, Juniper.

I looked around the room, spotting the cabinets. I ran over to the one that still had the doors attached. I pulled it open gently, hoping that it would not fall apart. It creaked open. Inside was empty, except for a shelf in the middle. I tried to pull it out, but it was nailed in. I bit my lip and tried to figure out if I could knock it out. I pushed harder and harder, but it would not budge. I tried to hype myself up, and then I hit the bottom of it with my knee. It moved slightly. I grabbed hold of it again and tried to wiggle it free, but the nails that held it in place would not release it from their grasp. I hit it again, slightly harder. Again, I felt it pulled out more, but not enough. I could wiggle it, but not enough to free it. One more, I thought to myself. I shifted my body to use more strength and swung, hitting the bottom of the shelf with the top of my thigh. I knocked it loose, and it banged against the cabinet.

I froze and listened, but could not hear anyone approaching. I let out a sigh of relief and yanked it out the rest of the way. I set it on the bottom of the cabinet so they would not see it if they came in, clueing them to my hiding spot. I stepped one foot in and scrunched down, squeezing myself into the confining space. As I adjusted to close the door, I heard Sienna's shrill laugh. I looked over at the door and saw her standing at the cusp of the doorway.

"Look at the little *Luna* trying to hide. If only Forest could see you now. How could he possibly think you are strong enough to be the Luna when you hide away like a child?"

She walked towards me. I tried to close the door, knowing that it was simply a deterrent at this point. She grabbed hold of it and ripped it off its hinges, sending it flying across the room.

"Do you really think a little door will stop me?" She jeered at me as she grabbed a fistful of my tangled hair and yanked me from the cabinet.

I fell out onto the floor and was pulled up on my knees. I screamed and held onto my hair, trying to pry it from her grasp.

Juniper, Forest reeled in my mind.

I could not respond. The only thing I could focus on was getting away from Sienna.

"I had hoped to make him suffer a little longer, but you are becoming a pain in my ass."

She grabbed the stuck drawer I had tried to open earlier and yanked on it several times until it slid open. My eyes darted towards the drawer, attempting to see what she was reaching for. The glint of moonlight shone off the sharp blade of a dagger, making my stomach drop.

"I've been waiting for this," she said through her sinister smile.

She pulled me up further, forcing me to stand.

"You don't have to do this, Sienna. You have your mate. You can leave now, run away with him. Live your life."

"Flint? Yeah, right! Have you seen him? He's not even a warrior. He can't take care of me. He's one of the weakest men in the whole pack. Why on earth would I want to be mated to him? Could you imagine our children? They would be the bottom of the barrel," she scoffed in disgust.

"But he's your mate?"

"Selene made a mistake! I should never have been paired with him," she screamed. "I have already told you. All I have to do is take you out, and Forest will take me back. I will be the Luna!"

She was completely deranged. She was so wrapped up in the story she had made up in her mind that she could not see the truth. I realized that there was absolutely no way to talk her out of this, so I prayed to Selene.

Selene, my mother, my goddess, please, keep everyone safe. Do not let anyone else die. Please keep Forest safe. Let him find love again.

My life was over, but I did not want it to end for Forest. He deserved to have a long and happy life. I could die happy if she could grant me that one wish. Sienna lifted the dagger above her head. I closed my eyes, not able to watch as she killed me. Her hand came downwards, slamming into my chest. Right as I felt the first sting of the impact, everything froze.

29

Juniper

E verything froze. I opened my eyes and was surrounded by a bright white glow. I must have died. Had I returned to Selene? As if on cue, the most stunning person I had ever seen walked out of the light and stood before me. She had a lithe frame with skin that looked like porcelain. Her eyes glowed the same blinding light that surrounded us, and her full, light pink lips looked like they had been sculpted. I looked at her body and noticed her pure white dress was made from the finest silk. She had long, flowing white hair that just barely touched the ground and seemed to move around her as if she were in water.

"Hello, Juniper," her ethereal voice echoed around us.

"Selene," I spoke her name as if I did not believe this could really be happening. "Am I dead?"

"Not yet, my child."

"Then what am I doing here?" I asked in complete bewilderment.

"You are a special child of mine. Your blood combines both of my creations. Your mother was bestowed with my power, your father, one of my children of the moon."

"Wait, what?"

"Your father was a shifter, a wolf. Just as your mate is."

"D-did she know?" I asked, stunned at her revelation.

"No. He was an Alpha traveling to the West Moon Pack to sign a treaty. His party stopped in Bellingham for the night. When he saw your mother walk into the restaurant, he was mesmerized by her beauty. They had their one night together before they both went on with their lives, but he had not known that she had become with child, with you."

I was speechless. My mind raced with thoughts and possibilities.

"So...I'm half shifter?"

"Yes. You are not the first. One of your ancestors was as well. Gladiolus Nary had grown close to the shifter who protected their village and had his child. She named her Iris. That child was one of your distant grandmothers."

"So I already had shifter blood in me?"

"Yes."

"Why are you here now?"

"With both sides of your blood coming together, you can harness more of my power."

"I don't think that can do anything for me now. Last I remembered, Sienna was about to stab me through my heart."

Selene smiled lovingly at me.

"I cannot help save you; you must do that yourself. I have only come to tell you about the possibilities."

"That's it?"

"Yes," she said softly, "use what you already have, my child."

What did she mean? What could I possibly do? I racked my

brain for every spell that I could think of. I could do a protection spell. Would that be enough to stop the dagger? It was all I could think to do. I looked back up to Selene, who had patiently waited for me.

"It is time, Juniper. I must return you to your body."

She stepped forward and gently grabbed my head, leaning forward. Her skin sent warmth and comfort through me, instantly calming my nerves. She kissed my head as a mother would her child. It epitomized happiness, like every good thing wrapped up in one touch. My eyes closed as I savored the sensation. My body felt like it fell from a cloud, and I was suddenly aware that I was back in the cabin, Sienna's dagger slamming into my chest.

The pain was unbearable. I grabbed at my chest, still feeling the blade embedded in my body. I could hear a loud howl nearby. Forest...he was here, but it was too late. I could feel myself dying. Sienna let go of my hair, and my body dropped.

"Dammit!" she yelled, looking back at the door.

I heard an explosion, and a light flashed through the open door. Sienna turned and ran, shifting back into her wolf. She left me there to die. Each breath is harder to take than the last.

I thought back to what Selene had told me. Do what I already could...

I gripped the dagger handle, contemplating whether I should pull it out. I let it go, knowing that I would only bleed out if I did. Not that I wasn't already, as evidenced by the ever-growing pool of thick crimson liquid around me. My fingers brushed against a necklace hanging around my neck. I inspected it with my fingertips. It was smooth and round. The moonstone! They must have put it on me after I used it with Mr. Burr. Could I use the same spell on myself? Was there time? I needed water... Would my own blood do? I needed the moon... My head rolled to the side, and I saw the dance of moonlight that had teased me earlier. I stretched my hand over, hoping to reach it. I could see the slightest sliver hit my fingers. I grabbed the moonstone with my other hand and began to chant.

"*Selene, mo mhàthair. Thoir dhomh do sholas gus an urrainn dhomh beatha a thoirt air ais don leanabh agad. Cleachd mi mar do làmhan, do shùilean agus do bhodhaig. Thoir do thiodhlacan don leanabh agad. Is leatsa mo chorp-sa airson a chleachdadh airson do ghnìomh.*"

With spit of blood coming out of my mouth, I gurgled out the words over and over, feeling weaker with each one. I coughed, tasting and feeling the blood fill my mouth. Outside, I heard another explosion. I could no longer keep my arm outstretched, and it went limp, losing the touch of moonlight. I had to keep trying. I hoped that I had it right, that this was what she had wanted me to do. My body could go no longer. I finished the last few words as the blackness encircled my vision.

Forest

THE BOND PULLED me straight to her. I could feel she was just over the ridge ahead of us when my scalp began to burn.

Juniper, I called out to her.

She never responded. If I felt her pain, then that must have meant that she was unable to hide from them. They had her. I had to get there before they hurt her again. We reached the top of the ridge, which gave us a clear view of an old cabin on the other side. My scalp still burned. We could waste no time.

Circle around. She's in the cabin. Kill anyone you find. I commanded my warriors as we started down.

I had gone only a few steps when I was knocked to the ground by excruciating pain in my chest. I pulled myself up, searching for her in my mind. I could see through her eyes as if it were a film over my own. Sienna was looking down at her with an unhinged expression. Her hair was wild, and she looked like pure evil. She looked down, showing me her chest. Sienna's hand was holding something. I tried to make it out...it was a handle. It...It was a knife. She stabbed her! She fucking stabbed her! My wolf howled in anger and pain for our mate. I had to get to her, to my Juniper.

I led the charge, and all of us were coming in full force. As we neared the bottom of the hill, there was an explosion to my right. I looked over and saw several of my men lying on the ground. I could not waste any time checking on them. I could feel Juniper's life slipping away. She was right there. I had to get to her. A brown wolf cut us off. Flint. The warriors beside me charged forward, biting onto his back and legs. The sounds of growls and jaws snapping faded behind me as I approached the cabin. Another explosion came from the other side. The bright yellow light from the flames lit up the sky. I ran around the cabin only to find Sienna standing in front of the porch, guarding the front. I growled at her to move.

"Not so fast, Forest," disdain dripping as she said my name.

"She held up some type of device in her hand.

"I know you don't know much about human contraptions, but this little thing right here," she held it up so I could clearly see it, "is the trigger for a bomb that Flint rigged to this piece of shit cabin. You take one step toward me, and your supposed little mate will be obliterated."

I could hear the rest of the warriors coming up behind me.

Stop, I commanded them.

I could not risk any more harm to Juniper. She was already slipping away; she would not be able to survive an explosion. I hesitantly shifted back to my human form, standing before her.

"Put it down," I used my Alpha command on her.

She would have to listen to it.

"Oh, no," she laughed at me. "See, as soon as I fled from your death sentence, I declared myself a rogue. I didn't want you to get any crazy ideas that you could force me into submission if a situation like this arose. Seems like it was the right choice.

"Now, listen up, Alpha. You are going to hear me out. Your little whore in there cannot be your mate. She's a fucking witch. There's never been a fated mate that was not a shifter. Our kind will only mate with another shifter. You need to get it through your thick head that she did something to you."

"You are crazy, Sienna," I gritted through my teeth. "Set the trigger down, and I will let you say goodbye to your parents before I rip your throat out."

"Tsk, tsk. You're not listening. I'm surprised you still believe that. If she really were your mate, you would have felt her die already."

Hearing those words out of her mouth made my stomach twist.

"What...? Feel like a knife is in your heart? Now you know what she felt when I stabbed her!" She screamed out.

The wolves surrounding me all growled at her, their hackles rising. The only thing stopping me from killing her right then was that I could still feel Juniper. She was hanging on, but it didn't seem that Sienna realized that. I needed to mess with her.

"Then you have nothing over us. You cannot kill her with your supposed bomb if she is already dead."

Her face flushed a deep red as her anger coursed.

"We'll see about that!" she screamed again.

She lifted her arm back up and slowly pushed her finger down.

"Stop!" I yelled at her, realizing my game had not played out as I hoped.

She was too far gone, lost in her own craziness.

"I don't think I will."

I saw her finger push down on the button. I raced forward, hoping to take her down before it connected, the others following my lead. The first sparks flew from the sides of the building, and my world moved in slow motion. I watched as the moss-covered boards that constructed the building began flying off. Another flash of light and a flame whipped out of a window. I raced past Sienna, only wanting to get to Juniper. I would rather die alongside her than live without her. I climbed the steps as a wave of heat hit my face. I was ready to give it all up when all of the sparks and flames sucked back into the cabin. Everyone froze as they watched. Juniper stepped into the doorway, her hands moving as if they were holding a globe.

"Juniper!" I called, not believing what I was seeing.

How was she alive? How was she walking? I could see the blood that was smeared across her skin and stained her clothing. Her eyes were closed, and I could faintly hear her chanting.

"*An teine a tha 'n taobh a muigh, thoir a stigh e. Cuir a mach e, cum a stigh e.*"

She pushed her hands together, holding them tightly as she repeated her chant. When she had finished speaking, she opened her eyes. They looked like what shifters would when their wolf was near the surface, but she had glowing silver eyes instead of the yellow/golden color most had, or even black, such as mine. I was taken aback. They were beautiful, captivating...

"Juniper..." I said again, needing to be sure it was her.

"Forest," she smiled as she raced to me, wrapping her arms around me.

The sparks from our bond flooded my body in a welcoming embrace. I pulled her tightly to me, feeling the need to make sure she was real, that it hadn't just been some figment of my imagination trying to convince me that she hadn't just died. Our lips collided, sealing the confirmation I needed. That it was, in fact, her. I had her, and she was safe. Her silver eyes dimmed, returning to the enchanting green of their natural color. I looked into them intently, finding myself lost in them.

"How is that fucking possible?" we heard Sienna spit out behind us. "She should be dead! I stabbed her! Don't you see what she is? What is she doing? Let go of me!"

We both turned to look at her as August and Atlas began to drag her away. She was thrashing in their arms, attempting to fight her way out. Her normally perfectly styled hair was matted and tangled, and her skin was coated with a thick layer of mud and dirt. She looked as crazed as she sounded.

"Stop," I told them.

I looked back at Juniper.

"I know that you disapprove of killing, but we cannot let her live. She will never stop trying to hurt you. If we bring her back now, there is no telling that she won't find some other person to tangle up in her web of lies, waiting to set her free, or even worse, come after you."

Juniper bit her lip. I could tell it was bothering her, but I waited for her to come to terms. She looked up at me with sad eyes.

"I understand."

I was shocked. I expected some argument or protest from her.

She lifted her hand to my cheek and continued, "Every time I tried to talk to her, she was lost. She had convinced herself of a story, and there was no way to break it. She used her own mate to seek revenge, not intending to stay with him. If Sienna and Flint felt an ounce of love for each other as I feel for you, none of this would have happened. I just ask that whatever you choose to do to her, I do not have to witness it. I have seen far too much already and do not wish to see more."

"I will take care of her," August offered.

I nodded at him, and they continued pulling her away. I had wanted to be the one to put an end to Sienna, but now that I had

Juniper in my arms once more, I could not leave her again. Sienna's screams began to quiet as they moved further away from us. I kissed Juniper again before stepping back, shifting back into my wolf.

Climb on my back, I linked her.

Once seated, we started our journey back home as a group, as a pack.

30

Juniper

"Did she seem angry with me?" I asked as Forest and I walked towards the cabin my Gran was staying at, the same one I had been at when I met him.

It was nearing sunset, and the sky was rich with vibrant colors above us, sending a warm glow down to the earth. We had been caught at the packhouse all day, debriefing on the events of the last few days.

"No, she seemed only to be concerned for you."

I nodded and chewed on my lip again, a trait I did when I was either nervous or excited. He reached out and took my hand in his, stopping me. I looked back up at him. After the events of last night, I would never let myself take what we had for granted. It was another reason I was so nervous to see my Gran. I knew I had hurt her when I did not return with Heather and Meadow two weeks ago. I was scared she was here to convince me to return, but I couldn't. I could not leave Forest. His pack was my home now; he was my home.

"Everything will be alright, I promise," he assured me.

I let out a sigh, trying to believe him. My Gran was like my kryptonite. She raised me after my mother had been murdered. She was essentially my mom. I saw how much losing my mom had affected her, how she lived in fear of it happening again. Now, I was about to go and confront her, telling her I was doing the same. I was leaving her. Forest gave me time to pull myself together before we walked up the front steps. I squeezed my fist a few times before finally giving myself the courage to knock on the door. I could hear shuffling around inside before the wooden door swung open. My Gran, after looking me over, grabbed hold of me and pulled me into one of her famous tight hugs. One where you felt that nothing could be wrong.

"Gran, I'm so sorry," I cried into her shoulder.

"What are you sorry for, girl? You have done nothing wrong," she cried back at me.

We held each other, sobbing into ourselves before we finally broke apart, wiping our tears away.

"What am I doing? Come in, come in," she said, ushering us inside. "I am so glad to see you, Juniper."

"I am happy to see you, too. How did you get here? Did you drive all this way by yourself?"

She laughed, "I did. After Heather came home without you, I knew I had to find you. She told everyone that you ran away. I couldn't believe it one bit and came to find you myself."

"What about Violet? Did she let you come?"

"Ha, that sister of mine is so full of herself sometimes. After the searching spell came up with nothing, she tried to tell everyone that either you had renounced your place within our coven or that you must have died. I knew that neither was true. She told me I couldn't come, and I told her where to stick it."

My mouth dropped at her confession.

"Won't they punish you when you go back?"

"I may have to do a few small things, but I know how to handle my sister."

We both laughed. She pulled us into the kitchen, where a soup pot was on the stove. She picked up the wooden spoon that was resting nearby and began to stir.

"I had hoped your mate would bring you to me today, so I made your favorite."

The rich, aromatic smell of earthy mushrooms, peas, and rabbit hit my nose, making me drool. Anytime I was sick or sad, she would whip me up a batch of her 'forest soup,' as she called it.

"Wait...are you okay with him being my mate?"

"I'll admit that I'm not thrilled with you being away from the settlement, but who am I to argue with a pairing curated by Selene?"

I could only smile. It had been a long time since I had seen my Gran this feisty.

"You two set the table. It's nearly ready."

We all sat down, enjoying our meal together. We recounted our stories from our time together and what had happened the previous night. When I came to the part where Sienna stabbed me, I divulged to both my Gran and Forest for the first time about my conversation with Selene.

"You mean to tell me that your father was an Alpha?" Forest asked, shocked by my confession.

"Supposedly, but I was so caught up with the whole 'being a shifter' deal that I forgot to ask her who he was."

"I think it should be easy enough to figure out. After all, you said he was coming to our pack for a treaty signing. We have all the records back home. We can look up what treaties were signed during the year of your...conception."

"Really?" I asked excitedly.

"Yeah," he smiled back at me.

My face lit up like the sun breaking into the day.

My Gran interrupted, "I find it so interesting that she chose a shifter out of all the men your mother could have found. There are not too many of either of our kinds in this world. Running into each other is rare anyway, but to find two individuals who happen to be visiting the same bar in the same small town at the exact same time...I half think that Selene had a little sway in that coincidence."

"Maybe so. I had never met a witch before Juniper," Forest added.

"It all makes sense now."

"What does?"

"I had never heard of a shifter mating with someone who wasn't one of their own. I just assumed it was the moon connection. But you're a half-shifter."

"I am," I said, fully processing the implications. "Do you think I can shift?"

"I'm not sure. If you haven't already, I would assume not."

"Yes, but she mated with you. Perhaps her newfound connection with the wolf side of her may draw it out," my Gran added.

"When do wolves usually start shifting?" I asked Forest.

I had been at the pack for two weeks, but I was still learning about their culture.

"We usually shift for the first time at the full moon nearest our sixteenth birthday. The full moon is next week. Maybe it will call your wolf out?"

"Maybe..." I said in almost a whisper.

"We can only wait and see," Forest said as he looked at me with wonder.

The rest of the evening turned out to be perfect. I don't think I could have been happier than I was at that moment. The two people I loved the most were sitting down, eating my favorite meal together, hashing out stories, and laughing. It was a moment I would etch into my memories forever. Growing up without my mother, I always felt like I had a close family, but I was unprepared to find Forest. With him, my life felt complete. I looked at him and smiled, watching him joke with my Gran. It was perfect; everything was perfect.

We left late that night. The moon, which was nearing full, shone its bright light down on us as we walked home. Forest had wanted me to ride him, but I wanted to spend as much time as I could just the two of us.

"Whatever happened with Sienna's mate?" I asked him.

"Flint? He tried to stop us. He barely lasted a few minutes before the warriors took him apart. I feel bad for him, really. I'm sure Sienna tricked him into helping her."

"She told him that she would be with him if he did," I added, recalling my conversation with him.

"I had no idea. I would have never been with her if I had known she had found her mate."

I didn't want him to know exactly how hard it had been for Flint. I could tell how guilty he felt already. Sharing it with him would only add salt to the wound.

"How are you doing with everything?" I checked in with him.

He let out a deep sigh.

"I'm processing."

"I'm sorry. I know you and Sienna were close."

"That's the thing. I don't feel bad about her. I'm just mad at myself for not seeing the situation. I was so blinded by the idea that no one in our pack would be bold enough to go that far that I wrote it off. Looking back on it now, I see all the red flags. Sienna's increasing obsession with becoming Luna, her reaction to finding out I had a mate. I mean, come on, she publicly threatened you. Even then, I didn't think she would actually follow through on it. That could have ended so much worse. I could have lost you."

He stopped and turned to look at me, regret shadowed on his face. I lifted my hand to his cheek, caressing the stubble on it.

"I was the one who gave her another chance after her threat. If I hadn't..." I trailed off and looked down at the dark earth below us.

"You were perfect," he said, putting his hands on my waist.

I looked up at him, surprised to see a soft and caring smile on it.

"I'm not so sure about that. I have so much to learn about shifters. Especially now, since I'm half shifter after all."

"You'll learn," he kissed my head.

Forest continued walking, helping me over the fallen trees and other obstacles. As soon as we returned to our apartment and closed the door, Forest pushed me up against the wall, colliding his lips with my own.

"Forest..." I moaned as his lips trailed down my chin, taking their time against my throat.

I ran my hands through his hair, pulling him closer to me. My breathing quickly became erratic as a deep burn inside of me traveled to my core. His hands caressed down my curves, grabbing hold of the loose cloth of my skirt. He hiked it up and spun me around so my hands supported me against the wall. He kissed across my shoulder, making my head roll back against his.

"I need you, Juniper," he said in that husky voice I loved so much.

"Then take me..."

At my confirmation of need, he nearly tore my panties as he pulled them down my legs and pushed me right there. I screamed out from the sudden but welcome intrusion. His movements were fast and desperate. He wrapped an arm around the front of my hips, pulling them to him, deepening himself within me. We both needed this—this primal connection to one another. I needed to feel him deep inside of me. My nails scratched the wall as he quickly built me up. From his deep breaths accompanying his grunting, I could tell that he would come at the same time as me.

As I felt a tingle go down my spine, quickly followed by tightening muscles, I came undone. Biting my lip so as not to let the whole house know what we were doing. He groaned against my neck as his final thrust pushed out the last of his seed.

We stood there panting for a moment before he slid out of me, turning me around to face him. His lips returned to mine, but instead of feverish movements, they were soft and precise. He hooked his hands at the back of my thighs and lifted me. I wrapped my legs around his waist, keeping our lips locked together. He carried me across the apartment to our bedroom, where he gently laid me down upon it. Our kiss only broke when he moved to undress me, followed by himself. Our two bodies were displayed to one another in all their natural glory. He looked me over as if I were the most precious thing in the world. I raised my hand to him, offering for him to come to me. No, needing him to come to me.

He climbed over the top of me, sliding in at the same time. He took his time, savoring every slope and curve of my body. At this point, he knew me in and out. Every like and dislike, and he made sure to please me to the fullest degree.

"I love you, Juniper," he said as we fought our conciseness for a few more moments with each other.

Right here. Right now. Not wanting to give up on our time, just the two of us.

"I love you too, Forest."

EPILOGUE

Juniper

I looked out the window as we drove through the small town I had grown up visiting throughout my childhood. We passed the small theater with its beige facade. I peered at the old ticket booth in the center and the letters that were barely hanging on to the sign. I recalled countless fits of laughter and even the stray tears I shed within those walls. The plain brick buildings on either side, with mom-and-pop stores struggling to stay afloat, draw only what the small local community spends. Next was the diner, where we ate every time we came into town, mostly filled with elderly people at this time of day... The nostalgia of returning was greater than the actual reunion. I had built up the town to Forest, telling him all about its grandeur, but now I realized how little modern updates it had. The town seemed to be disappearing before our eyes, just as the grandeur faded from my memories.

"How much farther?" Forest asked, snapping me out of my self-reflection.

"About thirty minutes."

We were on our way back to my family's settlement. The same property where I had spent my entire life until I had met Forest. I had no regrets and was thankful for the opportunity to return. An option I had not thought possible over the last few months. After meeting with Gran all those months ago, she had been working with her sister, Violet, to allow me to return to visit. They had been nervous to let me come back, knowing that I would bring Forest. We had never allowed visitors besides the occasional handyman or tradesman when work that we could not complete on our own was required. Even then, it was one of three men who had all been unknowingly vetted before they were allowed on the property.

Her winning argument was that I needed their support since I had failed to shift over the last few full moons. Even the memory made me wince. It was as if my body was trying. I was wracked with pain, feeling as if my body was trying to tear itself apart, only subsiding with the rising sun of the following day. Forest had been baffled trying to make sense of it. They had researched, looking for any other cases of this happening. Since one of my ancestors had been the same as me, I had reached out to my Gran again, asking her for her help. While I had always thought Violet a strong-willed woman who was not to be trifled with, we were still family, and she would not let one of her own be hurt.

"Turn right up ahead," I pointed, sitting straighter in my seat.

An overgrown and rough-looking dirt road peeked through the trees. Forest turned his black Range Rover Velar down the road, tree branches clipping its sides. We bounced in our seats as we traveled further into the surrounding forest. After another ten minutes, the trees began to thin, opening up to the cluster of wooden fairytale-like houses. We parked near the other cars closest to the road.

"Are you ready for this?" He asked me.

I laughed, "I think the real question is if you're ready."

He looked back up at the buildings. Women began to emerge from them, looking over at us.

"I'm going to have to be."

We exited the vehicle and started up the path.

"Juniper!" A scream came from ahead of us.

I already knew who it was. A mess of red hair flew through the other women who had gathered.

"Juniper!" She screamed again as she came bounding down the hill, crashing into me. I nearly fell over from the impact of her body, but quickly caught myself, wrapping her into a tight hug.

"Meadow, I've missed you!"

"Goddess, I have missed you too."

We squeezed again before we finally let each other go.

"You look a-mazing," she boasted, looking me over. "Look at these clothes."

I laughed, "Thanks."

She finally looked over at Forest and checked him out.

She leaned in and whispered in my ear. "He is delectable. Does he have any brothers?"

"Nope, sorry," I teased her.

"Darn," she whispered before turning to him.

"We've sort of met before; I'm Meadow," she offered her hand to him.

"Forest," he returned, shaking her hand.

She hooked her arm through my elbow and pulled me up the path. Forest followed closely.

"Come on, your Gran has been planning a little feast."

I could feel Forest's appreciation through the bond. Food was a quick way to his heart. When we neared the others, many of them walked up to welcome me back, but I could see their hesitance with Forest. Just as I had before him, most, if not all, of our coven had never met a shifter before. However, the stories I learned were that they were our protectors. I already knew that the unknown of a man who could turn into a beast would take a while for them to get used to. While they welcomed me back, they were not sure how openly they could talk to me with him around.

We were standing at the center of the settlement near the bridge, surrounded by a mix of women, when my Grandmother yelled, "Alright, the lot of you. You leave them be. They've had a long journey, and they need to rest. You all will get a chance to talk to them later."

I ran up to her and hugged her, "Hi, Gran."

"Hi, sweet darling. I'm glad to see you back."

"It's good to be back."

She smiled warmly at me before shifting her gaze towards Forest.

"It's nice to see you again, Alpha."

"You can call me Forest, and it's nice to see you, too."

We followed my Gran into our family house. The walls were lined with bookshelves and Victorian-style sofas, paired with the lingering smell of sage, which was welcoming to my senses. The rattling of pots and pans from the kitchen told me some others were already there. As if on cue, my great aunt Violet and several of my cousins came out, welcoming me back. After the slew of hugs and greetings, I introduced them all to Forest. Violet looked him over with hard eyes. I clenched my fists in worry, wondering how she would react to him. She walked up to face him, though her 5' frame was dwarfed by his towering 6'5" height. He seemed like a giant within our compound.

"Alpha, we thank you for saving our Juniper. We have much to discuss before this evening. Would you care to follow me?" She said in her austere tone.

Forest nodded his head and began to follow her to the study. I followed along with Gran, hot on my heels. We walked through the glass-paned double doors off the side of the living room, closing them behind us. Violet walked around the old French-style writing desk and sat in the deep purple velvet chair. Two other smaller chairs sat in the room opposite her. Forest pulled them back from the desk, offering them to my Gran and me before standing behind me.

"My sister has explained to me about Juniper's...parentage," she uttered with unease. "I understand that she may be a creature, such as yourself, but is unable to complete the shift?"

"That's correct. We have seen many of the characteristics of her being a shifter. Though I could find no other instances of a half-shifter and of what the implications of that are in any of our records."

"My grandmother told me a story when I was a little girl about the man who protected them. She described him as a large man who would scare the stray outsiders away from their village but was the kindest of them all. While in our coven, we do not usually know who our fathers were; she had told me that she always suspected that the same man, a shifter, who protected her village, was her father."

"She never told me such a thing," Gran said in surprise.

"It was in her later years when her mind began to stray." Violet said softly back to her before continuing, "I always thought that it was just that. An imaginative thought her wild mind had convinced her of. But if what Selene shared with Juniper is true, then I believe it may have been the case."

"Where did your grandmother come from?" He asked her.

"Our family comes from northern Scotland."

"The land of the first wolf." Forest thought out loud.

"So I've been told."

"Did your grandmother have shifting abilities?"

"Not that I ever heard, but her power surpassed all of her kindred. Perhaps she was capable of pulling more of Selene's energy with the closer bond to her."

"Wait, does that mean all of us Nary women have shifter blood in us?" I interjected.

"It would seem so," My Gran replied with a mischievous smile.

"Perhaps that is what drew the shifter to your mother," Violet added.

I hadn't connected the dots until now, but it would make sense. Especially learning how taboo it was for a shifter to be with a human. Since the revelation a few months ago, I had assumed it had been just a fling, but maybe there was more to it. A new can of worms had just opened in my mind, thoughts flying faster than I could keep up with. While I wanted to know more, I needed to focus on the present.

"Do you know what is happening to me?" I asked Violet.

"Only in theory," she answered as she clasped her hands in front of her.

"Which is?" Forest further questioned.

"You never had any shifter qualities while you lived here, correct?"

"Not that I know of."

"I think that when Alpha Forest marked you, as they call it," she said as she eyed him, "I believe he awoke something inside of you. Your wolf."

"Then why is it struggling to come out now? Will it ever?"

"You are talking about something from deep within you and pulling it out. I believe that perhaps, as a coven, we can help you with your transformation. When we draw the power in from it tonight, under the full moon, we will help direct the energy your body needs."

"I hope so. The last two full moons have been agonizing."

Gran reached over and held my hand. I gave a small smile over at her. I really hoped it would work. I did not look forward to another night of torture brought on by my own body.

After we met with Violet, I showed Forest around my room.

My childhood artifacts that lined the shelves and were plastered to the walls were like a window into my past. A whole wall of dried flower necklaces and crowns hung next to my full-length wooden mirror in the corner. My quilted bedspread that had my favorite stuffed animal propped up against the pillow sat centered in the room. A kaleidoscope of every color of the rainbow, paired with the natural wood of the walls and furniture, the sea of plants that hung near the window and across my shelves, was a welcome sight.

"Do you want to rest?" I asked Forest unsurely.

"Do you want to?" He smiled back at me.

"Not really..."

He stepped in, crowding the front of me. I could feel the warmth of his body against my skin. "Then what do you want to do?"

I bit my lip and looked up at him. I could feel his desire for me as I had for him, but our surroundings reminded me of where we were.

"The house is too small. We can't do it here. I'm not even sure what would happen if they heard us."

He kissed my head as he wrapped his arms around my waist. I took a deep breath, trying to reel myself in. If I could have had my way, I would have pushed him down on my bed, climbed on top of him, and ridden him until morning. But I had to remember why we were here. I placed my hand on his chiseled chest and stood on my toes, kissing him lightly.

"Later," I whispered through our lips.

He let a low grumble go from his chest, but stepped back. Instead, I took him through the settlement, showing him my favorite places. We only had a couple of hours, which were quickly consumed by conversations with the other women I had grown up with, who were mesmerized by my time away. We quickly found ourselves back in my room, preparing for the full moon gathering.

"Remember what I told you."

"I remember."

"Good, it is tradition. We do not shy away from nudity, as I know you're well accustomed to, but it will be different from back home. They are showing a substantial amount of trust in you, allowing you to be there."

"Should I...?"

I smiled at him. "If you want to. I think that they all would stare at you. Many of these women have never seen a man before. I'll check with Gran just to be sure."

I dropped my shorts, receiving an approving growl from Forest as his eyes traveled up the length of my legs. I could only blush as I finished undressing, standing before him. With such a temptation, he could not help himself. He made it to me in only two steps, lifting my body against his. His hands caressed my skin, and he peppered my neck with kisses. When his tongue ran across my long-healed mark, I shivered from the intense sensation. I was glad he had such a good hold on me; otherwise, I was sure my legs would have given out.

"Juniper, time to go," my Gran's voice called up the stairs.

He kissed me deeply before setting me down, still lost in a whirlwind of our desire. I huffed out a protesting breath and grabbed my robe off the back of the door before turning to leave. I could hear Forest chuckle behind me, making me squish my face together in rebellion. We walked down the stairs, finding my Gran and the others already waiting. I looked around, expecting to see Heather, but she was nowhere to be found. In fact, all day, I had not seen her. I was both happy and disappointed about it. What she had done to me had crossed a line, but deep down, I knew it was because she was trying to protect me and herself.

Gran had told me once, when we talked on the phone, that after she reported the compulsion spell she had cast on me, she was reprimanded severely. The coven questioned whether she would be allowed to travel again, a fear I knew she had about the situation. I hadn't heard any further news on the matter. I would need to check with Gran tomorrow about it. I did not want Heather to suffer because of the fate bestowed upon me.

We were a sea of shadows, our black cloaks flowing in the breeze as we walked down the path to the main hall. Forest had even worn a black button-up shirt with a pair of black slacks to try to adhere to our customs. Meadow walked next to me, having gabbed my ear off and filling me in on all of the coven gossip. I could only smile at her, loving the moment with her. Since I had returned, they decided to meet before the gathering as Violet needed to instruct the coven on what would happen tonight. We found our seats once inside, and the doors were closed, signaling the beginning of the meeting. Violet stood from her seat, hushing the whispers that flooded the room.

"Sisters, we welcome you tonight. Selene looks down upon us with open eyes as she sheds her light and power on us. Let us thank her."

She turned and raised her arms as she did every coven meeting, casting them at the large circular window.

"*Màthair, tilg do chumhachd nar cuirp. Bidh sinn a' caitheamh ar beatha dhut.*" We all chanted in chorus.

"Be seated, my sisters."

Violet stood and began addressing the room, "As you all know, tonight, our Juniper Nary has returned to us for the evening. She has brought her mate, Alpha Forest Woods, a wolf shifter from the West Moon Pack. Many of you only know of rumors about shifters. They are mated to one of their own kind, a bond forged by Selene herself and unbreakable. Juniper has discovered that the man who fathered her was, in fact, a shifter."

The room erupted in whispers as the gossip began to swirl. Gran had warned me that in order for them to help me, I would need to be honest with my heritage and embrace it in front of

them. I raised my chin, not allowing them to see my internal struggle. Violet quieted the room once more.

"While this is a new situation for us, we welcome them into
our coven. We will honor Selene's doings," she paused momentarily, gazing over the room. "With the revelation of Juniper's other
half, a child of Selene, she requires our help to bring forth her
transformation. Tonight, as we dance under her power, we will
help her. You may find your elder after the meeting if you have
further questions. Now we must move on to the next topic; along
with Juniper's return, Heather Nary will stand before us and her
accuser to receive her final judgment of using a banned spell upon
her."

My heart instantly began to race. I had no idea that this was
about to happen. I looked towards the back of the room. The
doors swung open, and two other women escorted Heather up. All
eyes watched as she walked to the front of the room, her head
hung low. I could only imagine how hard this was upon Violet,
passing judgment on her own daughter. I looked next to me at
Meadow, whose face was creased with worry. What would happen
to her if they exiled her, the known punishment for using a
banished spell?

"Heather Nary, you are accused of using a compulsion spell on
one of our own. Do you admit to your crime?"

"I do."

"Juniper Nary, we ask that you approach and face the accused."

I reluctantly stood and walked to the front of the room,
standing next to Heather. I looked at her, but she kept her head
down, never meeting my eyes.

Violet continued, "Juniper, as the victim of the crime, it is upon
you to pass judgment. What shall become of Heather Nary?"

I wished I had more time to prepare, but I could only follow
my heart.

"My situation is, well, new. Never before has a sister been

mated to a shifter. I believe that Heather, in her desperate need to protect not only me but also the coven, did the only thing she could think of at the time. While I disapprove of her decision, I forgive her for her actions, as I believe all those present should."

Heather lifted her head and looked at me, her eyes reddened from crying.

"Are you sure?" Violet confirmed.

"Yes. I believe the knowledge and the regret she will feel for the rest of her life is punishment enough. I ask that you pardon her for any wrongdoings."

The whisper mill surged as everyone gossiped about my request. I was sure no one would forget this meeting.

"So it shall be. Heather Nary, you are pardoned from your crime, but heed our warning. If you ever commit an act of treason such as this again, you shall be exiled from our lands and cut off from our coven's sisterhood."

"I understand," Heather said.

Heather turned to me, "Thank you, Juniper."

I smiled at her, and we retook our seats.

"Now that we have settled what was needed, it is time to celebrate the full moon," Violet said, gesturing toward the back of the room.

The doors to the hall opened, and everyone began to shuffle outside. The center of the settlement was decorated to perfection. Dried stalks of corn were fastened to the poles that hung the lights. Dried strawflowers decorated the tables, and a feast of all things corn was laid out on the tables. As Forest and I were finding our seats, Meadow and Heather came up behind us.

"I want to thank you, Juniper, and say sorry," Heather told me in tears.

I smiled weakly at her. "You're welcome...I am still working on forgiving you, but I will always love you. I hope that soon, in the future, we can get back the relationship we once had."

"I wish that too," she said back solemnly.

I meant every word I said. After experiencing the compulsion spell, I understood why it had been banished. She had taken away all of my free will. I was trapped in a shell of my own body, no matter how hard I tried to fight it. It was a betrayal on many levels. I did forgive her, but it would take time to come to terms with how it affected our relationship; one moment wouldn't fix it.

After everyone had filled their bellies with food, we began to gather around the bonfire. The full moon stood high in the sky, casting its luminous rays upon us. I could already feel my power growing, but the joy of the night was shadowed by the ache in my bones that had only grown the later it became. Violet stood center

"*Bidh sinn a 'dòrtadh nan ròsan ort Selene. Tha sinn a' tairgse dhut toradh ar saothair,*" she chanted and dropped her robe, stepping closer to the fire.

The other women of our coven followed suit, and we began to sing and dance around the flickering flames. I caught sight of Forest, who stuck to the tables, giving us the privacy to celebrate together. I caught his eye and smiled at him. Just as he returned the gesture, an explosion of pain hit me like a wrecking ball, and I fell to the ground. Forest was to me quicker than I could track. Another wave of affliction rolled through my body, making me scream to the heavens.

"It is beginning. Sisters, circle Juniper and link hands," Violet directed.

I could only faintly make out what was happening around me as my suffering debilitated my senses. Forest's touch and the sparks accompanying it were the only source of comfort or relief I could find. Through the pain, I could barely make out the rising voices as my coven chanted around me.

"*Leig às an tè a tha glaiste a-staigh. Thoir a-mach i gus am bi i saor airson ruith. Sian ar cumhachd dhut, mo Shelene. Thoir an cumhachd a tha a dhìth air ar piuthar.*"

Violet stepped forward as everyone repeated their words, touching my shoulder. I could feel the power flow entering my body as if waking every cell in its path. I heard the first crack of a bone; the same torturous feeling one would expect from it followed—another crack, followed by many more. My skin tingled as I watched red fur begin to push through my follicles. My hands, before my eyes, changed into paws. My face elongated, turning into a snout. I ran my tongue across my now-sharpened teeth. The pain subsided, and I stood on four legs. I raised my muzzle to the moon and howled a deep, ethereal sound. I could feel her within me. Selene was with me. I had shifted, becoming the person I was always meant to be.

AFTERWORD

Thank you for investing your time in reading The Wiccan's Hunt. Your support, whether through sharing with friends and family or leaving a review on Amazon, is greatly appreciated. Authors like me rely on readers like you, and your actions can make a significant impact.

Thank you again. To read more of Ayla's books or learn more about her current projects, visit her website at www.aylavolk.com.

Until we meet again...

PREVIEW THE WICCAN'S HUNT
BOOK 2 IN THE WICCAN SAGA

Juniper

My face peeked out from the icy cerulean blue waters, and I looked across the mirrored surface, reveling in the serenely quiet atmosphere. My legs slowly kept me afloat as I trod water in the middle of the lake that was surrounded only by the towering snow-covered mountains wrapped in a thick blanket of conifer trees. I turned my body, allowing it to float upon the stilled surface so that I could stare up at the clear blue sky. My arms skidded across the surface as I felt the pull of energy entering my body.

"Juniper," a deep, familiar voice called across the water.

I dropped my body back below the shelter of the water and turned to look at Forest, my mate, calling me from the rock-crested shoreline. I smiled at him and began to swim in his direction. The splashing of the water from each penetration of my arms and legs disturbed the peaceful quiet that I had been savoring, but with his appearance, I knew that my time hidden away at this sanctuary had come to an end. As I neared the shore, I cast a silent thankful message to the water for its retreat. My bare feet helped to steady me as I found my footing, lightly stepping over the icy stones into the plush white towel Forest held out for me.

"How many times do I have to ask you to bring someone with you if you come up to the lake?" he asked, slightly annoyed.

I lifted onto my toes and kissed him lightly on his stubbled cheek.

"That would defeat the purpose of coming out here," I said, smiling back at him.

"What would happen if a rogue found you alone so far away?"

"First off, I would hear someone coming long before they could get to me," I said as I began to walk back into the surrounding forest in search of the bag he must have brought with him.

I found it nearby, placed on a decaying, moss-covered fallen log.

"Secondly," I continued, "I stick to the middle of the lake. I can swim to the opposite shore if anyone comes."

He knew that this was a losing battle, but he never relented. He grumbled as he followed me over to the bag. I finished drying off and folded the towel, sliding it back into the small black duffle before returning to Forest, my smug smile never failing. He walked up to me and placed his rough, calloused hands on my bare hips.

"I will never stop worrying about you," he stated softly.

"And I know I will never stop worrying about you, but I watch you run off on patrol or perform your Alpha duties, but I trust you, as you should me. I would link you if I were ever concerned," I attempted to assure him while wishing he could see my side of the situation.

He let out a heavy sigh, "I know. I trust you; it's the rest of the world that I do not."

I kissed him again, feeling him tighten his grip on my skin as he gave in. As our lips parted, he leaned his forehead against mine.

"If we did not have things to do, I would take you right here. Watching you emerge with water dripping down your bare skin is driving me wild," he said in a husky voice.

I bit my lip as I felt a warmth course down my body.

"We shall make up for it later, then," I said in a sultry voice.

He grumbled his agreement.

"What do we have to do?" I asked, stepping back from him to curb my desire for him.

"Oakley found him. We have a phone call with him in an hour."

My muscles immediately tensed.

"We don't need to do this now if you want to wait," he added, sensing my demeanor change.

I took a deep breath and straightened my shoulders.

"No, I'm ready. I have spent my whole life wondering about him. It's time," I said confidently.

Forest gave me a deep, reassuring hug before stepping back and slipping his sweats off, sliding them into the bag with the towel. Without another word, we both shifted into our wolves, my petite red wolf contrasting with his towering black wolf. He leaned over and lifted the bag with his mouth, and we took off southward, back to our pack.

Thoughts of the man we were about to talk to filled my mind on the journey back. I had never thought I would find out who he was, as was typical for my upbringing in the Whisper Creek Coven. The women of my coven traveled into cities in search of prospective suitors to impregnate them, never seeing them again. As far as I knew, I would be the first witch since my family came to America over a century ago to meet her father. Six months ago, I found out that my father was, in fact, an Alpha, a message relaid to me from the goddess Selene herself. Forest and Oakley had been helping me track down who it could be since my arrival in the pack, and today was the day that I would finally find out who he was.

As we arrived back at the towering brick building that is our home, I shifted and grabbed the loose white cotton sundress that I had left on the nearby lounge chair. Forest did the same and slipped on the same sweats he had worn at the lake. We walked through the main entrance and found our way to Forest's office. Oakley joined us only moments later.

"How was the swim?" he asked with his usual cocky smile.

"It was good, thanks," I laughed back at him.

"Your disappearing acts are going to give our poor old Alpha here a heart attack one of these days."

"I don't disappear," I challenged lightheartedly.

"Oh please, you went to work in the greenhouse this morning, and when he went to pick you up for lunch, you were nowhere to be found. Do you know how complicated you make my day when my Alpha links me in a panic, and I have to search high and low for you?" Oakley chided.

"Well, I would tell him if he ever let me go alone."

"Hmm, I wonder why that is," he replied, implying heavily of the same reasoning Forest had told me each time I made my way out to the lake.

"Enough, you two," Forest interjected as he watched us from his desk, resting his chin on his fist.

Oakley, the Beta of our pack, and I had become close over my time here at the West Moon Pack. He was like the brother I never had, always teasing and razzing me. It was as if he had challenged himself daily to see if he could get a rise out of me, yet my years with Meadow had trained me well for someone with his personality. I mockingly squished my face at him before turning back to Forest.

"Get on with it, Oakley," Forest shifted towards him.

"Alright, you two know how long I've been going through the

old records, which, by the way, I think we need to digitize. I found the records of all meetings held around May 2000. There were two that happened during that month. The first was with the Burntwood Pack. Their meeting was on the first of the month, but they would have traveled from the north, not putting them in the states at all, let alone Mount Vernon."

"What about the other meeting?" I asked him.

"The Silver Ridge Pack. Their territory is in southwestern Colorado. That would put their route right through Mount Vernon."

"When was their meeting?" Forest asked him.

"May 14th is lining up pretty good as far as dates are concerned."

"What was their meeting about?"

"Alpha Caspian was a new Alpha and made the rounds to a few of the larger packs to establish relationships and solidify their treaties."

"Do we have a treaty with them?"

"Not an active one. As you know, there was the rogue epidemic in the late nineties and early two thousand. Many of the packs had treaties to provide support if needed. After the number of attacks lessened, many of those expired. Our pack has only kept up with the treaties with our neighboring packs, those in British Columbia and Washington," Oakley added the last part for my account.

I was still learning the politics of the pack. I had known that we had treaties with other packs as the Alpha from the Moon Fall Pack had visited around a month and a half ago to resign their contract with us, something done once a year. The North American packs were pretty dispersed. I learned of three in Washington state and several more in British Columbia. Most of the packs generally lived in Canada due to abundant land and space between human cities. Forest's office phone rang before we could get more details about the Silver Ridge Pack.

but they would have traveled from the north, not putting them in the states at all, let alone Mount Vernon."

"What about the other meeting?" I asked him.

"The Silver Ridge Pack. Their territory is in southwestern Colorado. That would put their route right through Mount Vernon."

"When was their meeting?" Forest asked him.

"May 14th is lining up pretty good as far as dates are concerned."

"What was their meeting about?"

"Alpha Caspian was a new Alpha and made the rounds to a few of the larger packs to establish relationships and solidify their treaties."

"Do we have a treaty with them?"

"Not an active one. As you know, there was the rogue epidemic in the late nineties and early two thousand. Many of the packs had treaties to provide support if needed. After the number of attacks lessened, many of those expired. Our pack has only kept up with the treaties with our neighboring packs, those in British Columbia and Washington," Oakley added the last part for my account.

I was still learning the politics of the pack. I had known that we had treaties with other packs as the Alpha from the Moon Fall Pack had visited around a month and a half ago to resign their contract with us, something done once a year. The North American packs were pretty dispersed. I learned of three in Washington state and several more in British Columbia. Most of the packs generally lived in Canada due to abundant land and space between human cities. Forest's office phone rang before we could get more details about the Silver Ridge Pack.

ABOUT THE AUTHOR

Ayla, a passionate reader and author of shifter and fantasy romance novels, is known for creating strong female leads. Her novels are not just stories but empowering journeys that delve into the strength women possess. Her character development is her strength, and readers will love getting to know them better and being able to invest their time into their tales.

Learn more about Ayla Volk and her books at
www.aylavolk.com

ALSO BY AYLA VOLK

The Stolen Heart

Warriors of the Eclipse

The Warrior's Calling (Book 1)

The Warrior's Bond (Book 2)

The Warrior's Proving (Book 3)

The Hunted (A Side Story)

The Wiccan Saga

The Wiccan's Alpha (Book 1)

The Wiccan's Hunt (Book 2)

The Wiccan's Circle (Book 3)

www.ingramcontent.com/pod-product-compliance
Lightning Source LLC
Chambersburg PA
CBHW052040240626
47153CB00006B/2165